Fourteen Spoons
Eight Stories

Fourteen Spoons
Eight Stories

Syrel Dawson

Library of Congress Control Number:		2016906329
ISBN:	Hardcover	978-1-5144-8624-5
	Softcover	978-1-5144-8623-8
	eBook	978-1-5144-8622-1

Print information available on the last page.

Rev. date: 04/19/2016

To order additional copies of this book, contact:
Xlibris
1-888-795-4274
www.Xlibris.com
Orders@Xlibris.com
738738

CONTENTS

To Lucas Mateo Dawson
May you always be enchanted by the stories you are told
and enjoy sharing the ones you have to tell

THE NECKLACE

The bells jingled as Mrs. Stern entered the tiny shop. Laura was so engrossed with her work that she barely looked up when she called out, "Just a second, I'll be right with you."

"No problem, my dear. I love looking over your handiwork, and I've no place I have to be. Take your time."

"Hello, Mrs. Stern. You are so kind." Laura returned her attention to the intricate safety lock that she was fashioning for her latest silver bracelet.

The smartly dressed woman with matching shoes and bag made her way to the first case of jewelry. Each single piece was unique and was made of antique buttons of every size and shape; the way the artist had joined them created either an image of nature or just a sense of harmony. Mrs. Stern moved to the next case. She smiled because these pieces were made of old typewriter keys. There were bracelets, necklaces, broaches, earrings, and cufflinks. Some were composed of random letters while others spelled words. She softly chuckled. "You know, Laura, I bet I could tell you from what company and which model each of these keys came."

"You're probably correct. You worked hard all of your life and always paid attention to details. I'll be with you in two shakes."

She returned to her work, and Mrs. Stern continued down the line of showcases in the narrow shop. Laura's work always delighted her. This group was filled with whimsical pieces of every color and material. The charm bracelets made of tiny plastic pieces caught her eye. "Oh, Laura, you're so creative! No one else would have thought to use old Cracker Jack prizes! I wonder if those boxes still have prizes. I've never seen my granddaughter eat any, so I don't rightly know."

"I couldn't tell you. My baby is a junior in college now!" Laura left her work area and leaned over to hug one of her favorite customers. "What can I do for you today?"

"I want to commission you to make another piece for me. I have a demitasse spoon that matches the teaspoon you made into a necklace for me. I thought my precious granddaughter would like and appreciate it."

"Do you really think she would as a five-year-old? Why do you say that?"

"She spent the night with me last Saturday so her folks could go to a wedding in the city. First, we played cards and then had coffee ice cream with jimmies and homemade sugar cookies. What happened next convinced me."

"Grandma, show me your spoon necklace again. I love looking at it," begged little Anna.

"Oh, my darling. I love looking at it too. Such memories! Let's go."

Hand in hand, Anna and Rebecca, her spritely white-haired grandmother, climbed the stairs to the bedroom with the big feather bed, which was piled high with beautifully hand-stitched quilts. Anna climbed onto the tall bed, nestled into the bedding, and cupped her tiny hands. "Ready, Grandma."

Rebecca opened her night-table drawer and retrieved a tiny key. She held it high to show her precious granddaughter and proceeded to the closet where the sacred box was kept. Rebecca could reach the box only by standing on tiptoes and stretching her arms way above her head. She hugged the box toward her chest and gently kissed the top.

"Here we are, my darling. Move over to make room for your grandma."

Anna scooted to her right, but not too far. She liked to cuddle up with her grandma because she always smelled of Breck shampoo and Lily of the Valley cologne. Rebecca put the prized box on Anna's lap. Together, they studied the finely carved wooden box. Rebecca slowly let her left index finger trace the grooved trim that framed the intricate scene of the Black Forest. Anna carefully imitated the movement of her special grandma and then watched her as she carefully inserted the delicate key into the lock and turned it so that the box opened. Rebecca sat straighter and smiled contentedly.

"Ready, Grandma. I'm ready to hold it carefully," whispered Anna.

"Oh, my sweet, sorry. I was just remembering. Here you go. Careful now."

Rebecca put the prized necklace into her granddaughter's hands. They were both so quiet that the coming in and going out of their breaths could be heard. Anna turned the pendant over and over before she brought it so close to her eyes that her pupils nearly doubled in size as she inspected it reverently. Finally, the silence was broken.

"Grandma, do you love this more than me?"

"Oh, my darling, of course not. I could not love anything or anyone more than you. If it were not for this spoon though, I would not have you to love."

Anna's confused eyes shot up, and she stared at Rebecca. "What do you mean, Grandma? The spoon is not my mommy or daddy."

Rebecca laughed until tears filled her eyes. "No, darling, it certainly is not human. It is a big, long story of long ago. And when you are older, I'll tell you. Right now, it is nap time, so let's lock this family treasure away and tuck up."

Anna replied, "Okay, Grandma. Thank you. I love holding it because you love it so much." She handed the necklace back and reached up to hug her grandmother and plant a kiss on her cheek.

"I love you millions, Grandma."

"Right back at you, my darling."

"Well, she obviously adores her grandma! I understand why she would like a necklace like yours. Those spoons must be pretty special to you, Mrs. Stern. When I made your necklace, I knew you were happy just by looking at your face. But you never told me the significance of the spoon, and I didn't feel I could ask. But now, we seem to be a bit closer."

"Well, it's a very long story."

"How about I make us a cup of tea and you can tell me if you wish. It'll just take a minute. Have a seat at my new table for special customers. I had been looking for an ice-cream-parlor set for my studio, and my older daughter found it at a flea market. Isn't it perfect?"

Laura went to the rear of the store to prepare the afternoon treat. Mrs. Stern continued working her way down the display cases, admiring Laura's silverwork. *There is nothing she cannot do. Such talent,* thought the older woman.

"Here we are. Have a seat now. I brought shortbread as well. I know you are a lemon-and-honey kind of girl, and that gave me an excuse to use my favorite honey pot," added Laura.

Mrs. Stern smiled at the lovely tray she had set. "You do things just the way I like them. Thank you."

Laura poured the tea into the bone china floral cups and placed a silver spoon on each saucer. Once both women had finished preparing their tea and enjoyed those first satisfying sips, Mrs. Stern put down her cup and reached for her handbag. She carefully opened the clasp, took out a small tissue-wrapped package, and handed it to Laura. "Here it is."

So as to protect its contents from falling, Laura gingerly unwrapped the parcel on her lap. When she saw its contents, she sighed. "Oh, this is just perfect for a little girl. A little demitasse spoon engraved with the same delicate rose—it's just like the spoon from which we made your necklace. Please share the story of the spoons with me."

"If you really want to hear it, my dear. But do promise me one thing."

"Of course, anything."

"If I go on too much, if you are bored, or it is too much for you—stop me."

Laura nodded. "I promise."

"I think it is easier to understand the spoons if I tell you what happened the day that my mama did not make my sister and me go to school."

Rebecca woke to the muffled sound of voices. It was her older sister, Hannah, and her mother. It puzzled her because they were dressed in nightclothes, sitting around a small dimly lit table in the middle of the night. She tiptoed into the kitchen, rubbing her eyes. "What are you doing, Mama?"

"Sweet Rebecca, what are you doing up? You need to be tucked up like a bug in a rug."

She rubbed her eyes more vigorously and yawned. "But what are you and Sissy doing?"

"Just some sewing, my little one. Some important sewing. Now use the toilet, wash your hands, and I'll come tuck you back in."

"Okay, Mama." Rebecca completed her bathroom tasks. She signaled her mother that she was all set and climbed back into the bed that she shared with her sister. Mama flowed into the room and sat on the edge of the bed.

"It is important that you get plenty of sleep and forget that we were sewing in the middle of the night. It is to be our secret, and there will be a wonderful surprise for all of us. Now, scoot down and let me give you a little kiss. I love you more than all of the stars in the sky, little one."

"I love you, Mama, more than—more than all the leaves and needles on all of the trees in the Black Forest." Their nightly ritual completed, Rebecca smiled, shut her eyes, and was instantly sound asleep.

After another hour's work of sewing tiny strong stitches, Mama and Hannah turned off the soft light and climbed into their beds to grab a few hours of precious sleep. All too soon, they would be able to see if their painstaking work would remain concealed.

"Mama, Hannah, wake up! The sun is up, and it must nearly be time for school."

While Rebecca's sister rolled over and moaned, Mama raised herself to her elbows and sweetly smiled at her younger daughter. "Oh, darling, I've a surprise today for you girls. No school! We're going on a trip. That is your first surprise. Now go and have a bath—"

"But it's not Shabbat!"

"No, but it is a special day. Have a lovely bubble bath, and there are some very special clothes on the sofa for you to put on. Now go, go. Give Sissy a few more minutes of sleep, and I'll make cinnamon toast and tea for us all."

Rebecca skipped to the bathroom with a broad smile on her face. A bath in the morning of a day that was not Friday was a delicious treat, and if Hannah was asleep, they wouldn't have to share the tub! She carefully plugged the hole, scooped in the precious bubble powder, and then turned on the hot water tap. Once the hot water tank was drained, she added just enough cold water so she could slip into the sea of bubbles. When she could hear the clatter of plates and cups announcing Mama was making breakfast, she called out, "Mama, where're we going?"

Mama popped her head into the bathroom and smiled that special smile. "Oh, it's a secret. That makes it part of the big surprise. When you're finished, drain the water and clean the tub so Hannah can have her own special bubble bath."

"OK, Mama." Wow! Two baths? This is going to be a special day, Rebecca thought.

Once she'd done as she was told, Rebecca headed for the sitting room to dress in the clothes that Mama had laid out for her. She had put on underwear, stockings, slip, and shoes when Hannah passed through to have her bath. "Morning, Becca. Maybe you should wait to put your dress on so you don't get cinnamon or crumbs all over it."

"Oh, good idea. Then I can really enjoy my yummy breakfast without being nagged." She ran to her sister and gave her a huge hug.

Once everyone had their fill of tea and deliciously decadent toast, Mama announced, "Finish dressing, girls. Nearly time to go."

Hurriedly, the sisters helped one another with buttons and bows, while Mama dressed in the bedroom. When she was ready, Mama opened the door and called, "Girls, come and each get your own satchel. We all have one to carry."

Becca and Hannah took the bag handed to each of them by their Mama and looked at her apprehensively. "Now, put on your best cloaks and we can head for the station."

Hannah nodded, and Becca looked at her sister and mother with an anxious expression, not moving. "It's okay, little one. All will be clear, but just do as I ask with no questions," assured Mama as she planted a kiss on Becca's head.

With that, the threesome was out the door, walking down the busy street toward the depot. The air was filled with loud trucks, blaring sirens, the sounds of steel-toed boots hitting the cobblestones, and sharply barked orders. A block before arriving at their destination, Mama put her bag down and faced her daughters. "Now, girls, when we go into the station, stay close. We'll be like actresses on a stage. Look happy and strong."

In unison came the reply, "Okay, Mama."

Becca found it difficult to do so as she looked around the large lobby. There were soldiers everywhere and Gestapo. She kept telling herself, Smile, be strong. Smile, be strong.

Before the little family reached Platform 18, a tall, mustached, pock-faced officer stopped them. "Papers, please."

"Of course, sir," replied Mama as she reached into her pocketbook. She pulled out the carefully folded papers that she had labeled "Aunt Gert's" and handed them to the intimidating man. Hannah grabbed little Becca's hand and held it in a sisterly fashion.

The officer glanced at the papers and from Mama to Hannah to Becca. "Why are you going there?"

"To visit my dear aunt. She is elderly and has pneumonia. We're going to care for her until she is strong again. Seeing the kinder will give her hope, don't you think?"

The uniformed man looked at the papers again, took a deep breath, and gazed at the threesome. He shook his head from side to side. "Who else can care for her?" he asked.

"No one, sir. We're her only family now. Please, we'll miss our train."

As the man looked down at the papers yet again, Mama slipped her fingers into her coat's inner pocket. He was so busy studying everything that he did not hear the faint tear of material. Mama removed a silver teaspoon, leaned over the all-important papers, placed the spoon on them, and said, "Look, it says here that she is ill and the commandant of her district asked that we come."

He looked directly at Mama, covered the spoon with his paw of a hand, and tucked it into his inner jacket pocket. "That will do. Make sure you follow all of our new laws. I'll check that you're back by this time." He pointed to the papers, handed them back to Mama, and turned on his heel.

"Come, girls. Quickly and quietly."

The sisters followed her through the gate onto Platform 18 and breathed a sigh of relief.

"Mama . . ."

"Not now, little one. Later. Remember, no questions."

The steam train pulled alongside the platform noisily, and the family entered the third-class carriage. At the far end, they found two seats facing two. They piled their satchels onto the fourth seat in hope that no one would try to claim it and plopped into their seats. The whistle shrilled and the train pulled out.

"Mama."

"Soon, darling, soon."

The train gathered speed as it left town, and the click-clack became louder. No one sat in the next set of seats, but beyond that, the carriage was filled.

Mama leaned forward toward her cherished daughters and began to whisper, "This is our only hope of leaving what Germany has become. We're going far away on a special trip. Tell no one about the silver spoon. We need to keep secrets this time and be award-winning actresses in order to stay safe. Listen to me, my dears. Trust me. I'll try my very best to keep you from harm's way because I love you."

All the girls could do was nod at their mother with serious faces and silent lips.

The train wended its way through several villages and headed for the forest. The girls stared out the windows of the carriage, not really seeing the variety of trees, the woodsmen signaling one another, or the multitude of deer grazing. The rocking of the train soon lulled them into a shallow sleep. Mama looked at her girls and mouthed a silent prayer, asking for the little family's safety.

The relative quiet was shattered as the door nearest them was shoved open by a tall guard who barked, "Papers, everyone. Papers. Have them ready for inspection. Now!"

The girls sat up straight and looked at their mother, who put a finger to her lips as she reached into her bag yet again. When the pair of soldiers reached their seats, the higher-ranking officer extended his hand without speaking. Mama placed the papers on his palm with a sweet smile, and the girls stared at their shoes. A few tiny tears began falling from Becca's chocolate-brown eyes. Mama leaned forward, pretending to adjust the buttons of her sweater, and whispered, "Strong. Be strong, my little Shirley Temple."

Becca rubbed her eyes, and Mama smiled and leaned back. Seeing that the officer was too interested in what had happened, Mama volunteered, "My little one is a sleepy little girl who can never button her cardigan correctly."

The tall man allowed a smile to creep across his face. "I have one just like her at home. It is tough to get them straight, isn't it, little one?"

"Yes, sir," Becca whispered.

He laughed and tousled Becca's hair. And as he handed back the papers, he said, "You're fine. You change trains next stop. Just walk across the platform."

"Thank you. We'll be ready."

The officer lifted his hand in a little wave and was off.

As the train slowed, Mama had the girls adorn their cloaks and gather their satchels so they could disembark easily and confidently at the station. Although the screech of brakes and frantic calls of passengers were deafening, the family was able to step onto the platform and cross it without trouble. The next train was already there waiting for them. Mama opened the door to the carriage but was blocked by a burly guard with a thick gray mustache.

"Papers! Show me your papers."

"Certainly, sir." Mama put her bag down and reached for the documents. As he perused them, she deftly and unobtrusively tore at stitches in her

dress hem and removed another spoon. She nodded at Hannah, who then followed suit.

"These papers are not in order. The numbers are all wrong."

"Please, let me see where you are looking," requested Mama demurely.

He tipped the folded papers toward her and pointed. Mama extended her hand and carefully placed a teaspoon in the appointed place. Lightly tapping it, she looked at the man earnestly. He grunted. "Well, they're nearly correct," he said and waited.

Hannah quickly placed a large serving spoon in her mother's other hand. "If you look here, sir, I think you'll find what numbers you need." Mama quickly covered the smaller spoon with the larger.

"Ah yes, madam. You're quite right. Welcome aboard."

The story was rudely interrupted by the jingle of the bells on the shop door. *Dang it,* thought Laura. She looked at Mrs. Stern and rose to see who had the audacity to walk into her shop at that very moment. Fortunately, it only took a few minutes to sign for the packages that the FedEx delivery man had brought; but when she returned to the tiny table, her friend's eyes were closed. Laura was not sure if she was sleeping, so she gently reached out to touch her cheek.

"Oh, I must have nodded off. I'm so sorry."

"Nothing to worry about at all, Mrs. Stern. I've tired you out, and I'm sorry for that, but not for receiving the gift of your story. I'll gladly make the necklace for your Anna and bring it to your house on Friday. I know the necklace will be cherished."

"Thank you, my dear. I do hope I didn't bore or scare you," she added as she rose from the petite table and chairs.

"I truly feel blessed that you trusted me with so much of your family's history. And if you are up to it, I would love to hear about the rest of your escape when I deliver the necklace on Friday."

Mrs. Stern made her way to the door, opened it, and turned to Laura. "Only if you call me Rebecca!"

"Deal! Rebecca, see you in a few days." Laura slowly closed the door, completely lost in thought and admiration for such a remarkable, unassuming woman.

Friday arrived and Rebecca baked rugelach with her granddaughter in preparation for Laura's visit. The best china teacups and pot were set on a tray that had been covered with a white linen lace cloth and neatly pressed matching napkins that little Anna had carefully folded.

"I love coming to stay with you, Grandma. I love helping you make things and hearing how you used to help your mama when you were my age," Anna said and smiled.

"I love sharing with you, but right now, I think you should tuck up for a wee sleep before my friend Laura arrives. I want you to be bright-eyed and bushy-tailed."

"Oh, Grandma, you always say that! I never wake up grumpy, do I?"

"No, darling, you don't. Let's go now."

Together, hand in hand, they climbed the steps to Rebecca's room. Anna kicked off her shoes, jumped up on the big bed, and pulled the soft pillow from under the bedspread. She squeezed it to make an indentation for her head and snuggled down. After receiving a multitude of kisses from her grandma, Anna yawned and shut her eyes.

Rebecca tiptoed downstairs to finish the tea preparations and to search the crammed bookshelves in the sitting room for the scrapbooks that would help Laura understand the journey of the spoons. *There you are,* Rebecca thought. *Search over.* She stretched to the top shelf and reached for the well-worn book. She retired to her overstuffed velveteen chair and ottoman, threw the handmade afghan over her knees, and turned on the reading lamp with the tasseled shade in the same rich green as the chair. She lightly traced around the edges of the leather cover and sighed. "Such a long time ago," she whispered to herself and began thumbing through the pages filled with memories. Soon she joined Anna in dreamland.

Rebecca was not sure how long she had been sleeping when the sound of the doorbell roused her. "I'm coming! Hold on," she called as she shuffled to the door, still in a sleepy fog.

"Hello, Mrs. Stern. Were you not expecting me?"

"Rebecca, remember! Of course I was, dear Laura. I was just snoozing in my chair and thought the doorbell was part of my dream. Forgive me for keeping you waiting. Do come in."

Laura pecked Rebecca's cheek and passed into the cozy sitting room. "I hope you like it. The demitasse spoon was delicate and took a little patience and a lot of ingenuity to get that tiny rose on the bowl to lie flat."

"Have a seat here on the sofa. I am sure it'll be perfect. Let me put up the kettle for a pot of tea. Anna and I baked some fresh cherry rugelach for a Shabbat treat to go with it. She's with me for the weekend again, so you'll meet her."

"That would be lovely. Can I help?"

"No, it'll take me only a few minutes. Be right back. My precious granddaughter is napping, but she'll wake in a half hour or so," Rebecca replied, beaming.

While the tea was brewing, Laura looked at the family photos that were so proudly displayed on the far wall. *Many generations of much-loved people,* she thought to herself. *I wonder if this was Mrs. Stern when she was a wee one.* She glanced at the modern framed school photo on the end table. *If that is she up there, she looked just like her little Anna.*

"Oh, you've found my family," Rebecca remarked as she carefully placed the tea tray on the coffee table. "So many memories. That is me with my older sister, Hannah. May she rest in peace. It was right before we finally escaped from Germany. Now looking at it, I can see the tiny bulges in the hems of our dresses where Mama sewed the spoons. I guess none of the Gestapo had seamstresses in their families because they never saw them. Come sit. We'll toast my mother of blessed memory with tea and her secret rugelach recipe."

Laura took her seat and allowed her hostess to pour her a cup of tea and pass the plate of pastries. "Oh, delicious!"

"Thank you, my dear. Now let me see your artistry."

Laura put her cup and saucer down and bent over to reach into her large tote bag. She removed a small white box labeled "Old Nouveau, Paris Back Studio" that was tied with a blue satin bow. "I do hope you like it. Please, please tell me if you want anything changed. I want it to be perfect."

Laura handed over the box and pulled her hands toward herself, palms together and fingertips to her lips. She held her breath as

Rebecca untied the ribbon, opened the box, and gasped as she looked at its contents. She was stunned into silence.

"What do you think?"

"Oh, my dear. It is perfect! Just perfect." Carefully, she lifted the new necklace from its box with one hand and pointed at the details with a finger from the other. "Oh, Laura."

"I put it on a blue satin ribbon for now. I thought it more appropriate for a young girl. Perhaps when she is older, we can switch to a silver chain."

The patter of little feet broke the silence, and the box was handed back to Laura to be reassembled. "Grandma, I woke up and heard voices."

"Come here, dear girl, and meet my friend Laura. She has made a surprise for you."

Anna ran into her grandmother's open arms for a hug and a kiss on the top of her head. Then she turned to Laura and managed a tiny "Hello, I'm Anna."

"Hello, Anna. I'm so happy to meet you. Your grandma is one of my most favorite people in the entire world."

Anna smiled. "Mine too."

Rebecca giggled and said, "Well, now that you two have that established, let's see what Laura has for you."

Laura handed the little box to Anna. "Here you go."

"But it's not my birthday."

"I think we'll call today Grandma and Anna Day. Now that calls for a present, doesn't it?" declared the elderly woman.

Anna nodded in agreement and turned her attention to the box in her hand. She put it on the coffee table, untied the blue bow, and lifted the cover. She stared at the contents, looked at the two adults, and then gently lifted out the necklace. Her eyes grew as big as full moons, and her mouth dropped open. "Grandma, it is a mini version of our treasure." Anna pulled it closer so she could inspect the details of the spoon. It even had a tiny rose on the bowl, just like her grandmother's necklace.

"Let me tie it around your neck, Anna," offered Laura.

Anna ran over to the jeweler and turned to face her grandmother while the necklace was secured.. Immediately, she ran upstairs to the bedroom so she could look in the full-length mirror. From the door, she called, "Grandma, come put on your necklace too."

Mrs. Stern climbed the stairs, glided into the bedroom, fetched the key, and reached high on her tippy-toes to take down the precious box. Once opened, she removed the spoon necklace and slowly put it on. She touched the spoon and looked down at Anna, who was smiling from ear to ear. Together, hand in hand, the grandmother and the granddaughter moved to the freestanding mirror. They gazed at their image silently but contentedly.

Laura stood in the doorway and studied their reflection and knew the generations to come would never forget the story of survival and love.

Did I Do That?

Benny dragged his feet as his family entered the third gallery of the city's art museum. Saturdays were not meant for looking at wicked old paintings by artists he had never heard of. He really wanted to be outside throwing the football in the backyard and jumping into the piles of dry autumn leaves that had been shaken loose by last night's storm.

"Who wants to look at portraits of scary-looking people who stare right back at you?" he complained.

His dad tried to encourage him. "Come on, Ben. There's bound to be something you like here. This gallery will have paintings showing lots of action. It was like before cell phones took pictures. People had to bring their personal artists with them to picnics and dinner parties if they wanted a visual memory."

"Yeah, right." Benny followed his folks with head hung low. "Look," he cried, pointing at the clock hanging above the far door of the gallery. "It's three forty-five in the afternoon. Who wants to look at pictures of parties and Christmas and picnics on the banks of some stupid French river at 3:45 PM when you could be outside?"

Benny liked action, and he especially loved sixth grade and Mr. Grant's social studies class. He made everything seem exciting, and Ben often felt he was right there with whatever Mr. Grant was explaining. He remembered that Mr. Grant did his senior project in college on a bunch of paintings that showed the insanity of the Salem Witch Trials. Now going to Salem Witch Museum might be cool.

"Hey, Dad, do you think—" Benny stopped dead in his tracks. His folks were staring at a painting, as usual. "Hey, Dad." Benny looked from his father's face to his mother's. They were silent, looking attentively straight ahead with their mouths hanging open.

"Oh my god," his mom whispered. "I didn't get that the Civil War was this violent."

Benny was confused by what his mother had murmured and turned to look at the artwork that captured her interest. He was silenced by the expansive painting of a troop of soldiers, mere boys, after a Civil War battle. There were a few men with smart uniforms standing and directing the activity of those few who were frantically trying to save the dying or comfort the wounded.

"Oh, wow! I bet that is the Battle of Shiloh. Mr. Grant told us all about it. Look at all of those hurting soldiers! I wonder who's washing their wounds and why some of the men are just standing around, watching, while some dudes are dying. I don't get it. If I were there, I'd—"

Suddenly, Benny felt lightheaded. He rocked back and forth and grabbed his dad's arm to steady himself. His dad looked down as Benny's eyes rolled to the back of his head and he slumped to the floor. He cried "Benny, Benny, what's wrong?" as he gathered his son into his arms and plopped him on the bench in the center of the gallery.

"Benny, Benny, what happened? Are you okay? Benny, wake up!" his mother called frantically as she stroked his clammy face.

Slowly a stream of diffuse light left Benny and headed toward the painting and disappeared. His folks were too engrossed in waking him to notice the beam. Holding on to their son, they heard what they thought was his voice coming from somewhere behind them, but it was muffled.

"Mom! Dad! Get me out of here! This isn't funny! I will go to any museum with you, whenever you want, any time. Just get me back!"

Their eyes drifted up to the painting of Shiloh. They didn't seem to notice the movement near a bush in the painting. Branches parted and staring at them, calling for help, was Benny in his jeans, high tops, and a sweatshirt complete with the bulge of a concealed water bottle. They watched without seeing their son as he took out his cell phone from his back pocket and tapped the screen. Mr. Landon's phone began to vibrate, and he grabbed it and slid it open. He thought he heard Benny say "Dad, Dad, look at me. I'm up here. Get me out! The cannons are beginning to fire again." Mr. Landon shook his head, stared at his phone, and then looked back at his son coming to on the bench.

* * *

General Ulysses Grant moved closer to Benny. "Who may you be? That is not the uniform of any regiment I know. Be ye a Yankee or a Rebel?"

He reached out to feel Benny's shirtsleeve and then his jeans. "What are these, boy? Speak up now."

"My clothes! My jeans and sweatshirt, sir."

"Jeans? Sweatshirt?" The general shook his head. "From where do you come? To which regiment do you belong?"

"I am not from any regiment. I am not from now."

"Now? Where is Now? Stop talking nonsense, boy. Who are you?"

"Benjamin Landon, sir. I am from the town of Tulsa."

"Tulsa? Where would I find that?"

"Oklahoma. Tulsa, Oklahoma."

General Grant just shook his head and called out, "Hey, Dr. Scott! Hey, Doc! You better come over here. I think this one has lost his mind."

"General, sir. Please. I just want to go back to my parents."

"That is what I am trying to do, son. Just tell us from where you come!"

"Tulsa, Oklahoma. But I'm not from 1862. I'm from the future. I'm from 2016. I was looking at this painting and then *whoosh*. Now I'm in it with you."

General Grant looked distressed. He held on to Benny and then bellowed, "Doctor, get over here, now!"

A rather rotund man in a Union uniform waddled his way past injured soldiers calling for help. He hated having to report to the general instead of attending to the wounded men on the field. "Yes, General?"

"This peculiarly dressed young one is a little confused. He says he is from someplace called Tulsa, Oklahoma. He says he fell into a painting and that he is not living in the year of our Lord, 1862, but in the year 2016."

Both men roared with laughter, but then they looked at each other with concerned eyes. The doctor nodded then spoke, "Now, son. Where is home? Tell me all about yourself."

"My name is Benjamin Landon, and I live in the city of Tulsa in the great state of Oklahoma. Where I live, it is 2016, and I was visiting the city art museum with my folks. And I fell into this painting of the Battle of Shiloh, and here I am."

Before the good doctor could respond, cannonballs started flying and exploding near them. Some men shouted orders, and those who were hit screamed in pain. General Grant picked Ben up and ran toward a thicket that was fifty feet behind with the doctor following at a quick trot. He gently placed Ben on the ground and lay on top of him to shield his body. After what seemed like hours, Grant sat up and whispered, "I think we are safe now."

"Sir, look. I need to get out of this picture. I mean, I need to get back home. My folks are going to go crazy if I don't. You need to help me."

"Son, you must've been hit on the head. You tell us you're from a place of which we have never heard. Think clearly. Where do you live, and we will get you there as soon as we can."

The doctor put his arm around Benjamin's shoulders in a fatherly way. "Now, young Benjamin, I know this is difficult for you. Just shut your eyes, relax your body, and think about your parents. Think when you last saw them . . . think about what is around your home. Pine trees? Fields of crops? Great woods?

Trickling stream? Shops in a town? Don't say a word. Just picture it. Once you see it, let the words flow."

Ben did as he was told. He slumped against the doctor and breathed deeply until the sounds of muffled jazz sprinkled the air. The doctor and General Grant looked fearfully around them. "From where is that sound coming?" asked the general.

"It seems to be emanating from young Ben's pocket," whispered the doctor, pointing to Benny's back pocket.

Instantaneously, Benjamin was jerked from his trance. He reached into his pocket and pulled out his phone. He hit ANSWER. "Hello?"

"Ben, is that you? Your voice sounds funny. Maybe it's a bad connection. Anyway, this is Mr. Grant. I just wanted to congratulate you on an outstanding project. You made the general come alive in that mock interview you wrote, and you even showed the kind side of him that so few knew. Listen, are you there?"

"Yes, Mr. Grant. I hear you," Ben replied, scratching his head. "You wouldn't happen to—"

"Ask me on Monday. What I wanted to tell you is I have his belt buckle. General Ulysses S. Grant was my great-great-great-uncle, and it was passed down—"

"You have what? But I can see it on him right now. Right now."

"Good imagination, sport. Would you like to wear it on Report Day?"

"Ah, cool. Would you like to talk to General Grant? Like now?"

"If I could time travel, I—"

General Grant tore the phone out of Ben's hand. "Young man, I know not what this is, but it is causing you to talk outlandishly." Grant reached back with his arm and threw it with the speed and distance that would have pleased any baseball player. "Now concentrate and do what the good doctor has asked," he commanded.

"But-but my cell . . ."

One stern glare from the general sent Benny back to the task handed to him. He began by thinking of his house but then switched to where he last remembered being with his folks. *What was happening when I got so dizzy and went poof? What was it? Maybe that will help in some way.* He squeezed his eyes tightly shut and clenched his teeth in concentration. Random thoughts filled his mind, but then he focused in on standing in front of the painting and being disturbed that not everyone in the Battle of Shiloh was helping those injured.

"That's it!" He broke away from the two concerned gentlemen and ran to the nearest soldier in distress. He was lying on his back, moaning. "Water, water. Thirsty. Just a sip, please."

Ben knelt down and pulled the injured man onto his lap. He reached in the pocket of his sweatshirt and pulled out the bottle of water he had so expertly hidden from the museum guards. He twisted off the cap and gingerly tilted the bottle toward the parched lips. "Here you go, soldier. Drink slowly so it will stay down."

The injured man could not manage to gulp. Benny spied a silver teaspoon engraved with a rose in the soldier's pocket. He gently removed it so as not to hurt him and used it to spoon drops into his mouth.

The doctor and the general ran toward Benny. "Stop, Ben. Stop. He's a rebel and may harm you."

"It's okay. He's just a hurtin' soldier. Not much older than me!"

The injured soldier opened his eyes, looked at Ben, and whispered, "Thanks for your kindness." Then he closed them again. Ben shrugged his shoulders, not knowing if the young man was sleeping or dying. He then carefully lay the soldier's head on the scraps of grass, replaced the spoon, and rose as the doctor and general reached him.

A familiar lightheadedness began to creep over him. As Ben started to keel over, he saw General Grant's belt buckle shining in the sunlight. He managed to get out a "Take good care of that belt, General Grant! I'll need it on Monday" before disappearing into the mist.

* * *

"Ben, where have you been? We were worried sick about you. Did you wander into another gallery? After you recovered from that dizzy spell, we thought you were walking with us into the next gallery, but then you seemed to vanish," exclaimed his mother. "We came back to look for you but never thought we'd find you sitting on the same bench, looking at the same painting."

"Mom, what time is it?"

She pointed to the clock. "It's 3:50. Why?"

"Just wondering. It's only been three minutes? What do you think of the painting of Shiloh? Don't you think it looks so real that it could come to life?"

Ben pointed at the painting, and his eyes opened wide as saucers. "Look! It's different! General Grant is kneeling and giving the soldier water from his own canteen. He was standing a minute ago. The soldier is holding the spoon I used. Oh my god! What did I do?"

His parents exchanged glances and shrugged. "Son, I think it's time we stopped in the café for a snack. Maybe your blood sugar is low."

His parents headed for the gallery exit. Ben followed, walking backward, never taking his eyes off the painting.

The Perfect Apartment

"Look, I know you want to be Miss Independence, but it is really expensive to get set up in an apartment of your own. We all started by scrounging through grandparents' and neighbors' basements for bits and pieces. No one starts off with matching dishes, shiny pots and pans, and pristine bedding. Your aunt says she wants to help, so take her up on it."

"Will it make you happy, Mom?" an exasperated Jen asked.

"Yes." She pushed her salt-and-pepper hair back from her face and smiled at her daughter. "Not only do you have your aunt's auburn hair, you seem to listen to her and share jokes I just don't understand. If I hadn't been there when you were born, I would have thought she were your mother, not me."

"Okay, okay, I'll go over."

"And bring boxes!"

Jen headed for the basement in a not-so-quiet manner, showing her true feelings about being the recipient of old junk for a new adventure. She knew her mother was right, especially since her salary as a first-year preschool teacher would barely cover her expenses, but she didn't want to look like she shopped exclusively at the Salvation Army store. Finding boxes wasn't a problem, but making sure they fit inside one another was. Her 2005 VW Bug didn't have much room for stuff. When half a dozen boxes had been retrieved, she headed for her car and her aunt's house.

Aunt Susie was her favorite relative, and Jen always had a good laugh with her. When Jen's mother didn't get her, Susie did. Unlike her family, Susie had lived in the same house for all sixty years of her life. When Jen's grandfather died, Susie bought her siblings' shares of the family home. She claimed that there were spirits in the house, and she didn't want them disrupted or upset by new owners. If Susie was ever to marry, it would be under the condition that they lived in that house.

Jen rapped lightly on the back door and walked right in, as always. "Aunt Susie? Aunt Susie? Where are you hiding?"

"Down in the cellar. I started pulling some things out for you. Come on down, but careful of the bottom step. It's a little wobbly."

"Do you want me to bring down some coffee?"

"Not yet, we'll take a break later. I made your favorite cinnamon rolls, and they need to cool a bit.

Jen headed down the stairs with her arms full of empty boxes. "Auntie, you are the best," she called as she walked through the warren of tiny rooms that made up the basement of the hundred-year-old house.

Susie looked up from the storage closets at the far corner of the last room. "You aren't so bad yourself. I found some great stuff for your very first apartment, and it isn't chipped or cracked. Come over here."

Jen's aunt was surrounded by stacks of assorted dishes and Pyrex casserole dishes. As Susie moved over to make room for Jen, she pushed back her auburn hair, which was showing wisps of gray roots behind her ears. Susie threw open her arms, waiting for a hug from her favorite niece, and Jen obliged with a tight squeeze.

"Where did you get all of this, Auntie Susie?"

"Oh, some of it was your grandparents'. I think those pots down there may have been from your mother's first apartment. Some of it—well, who knows? This house seemed to be a home for a lot of people through its life. Some people stayed months and years. Others just passed through. Let's get started."

"Look, there is dinnerware with place settings for four here. I know the cream color with green ivy is a bit old-fashioned, but I'd guess it was never used. I think I remember Gran collected it from a bank. They had this deal going where whenever you deposited $50, they gave you a place setting."

"Banks did that?"

"Oh, they used to really look for customers." Looking at Jen quizzically, she asked, "Well, what do you think?"

"It isn't bad. Dinner plate, side plate, bowl, cup and saucer for four. There's enough to have two guests for dinner. I guess I can live with it until I'm rich and famous!"

Jen carefully wrapped each piece in the old newspaper that Susie had brought to the basement for just that purpose and placed it in the boxes. She knew the saucers would never hold a cup; that would be way too old-fashioned. When she finished, she moved the boxes to her aunt's kitchen and scooped just enough coffee grounds into the paper filter for the cone of the old Braun and flipped the button.

Taking two steps at a time and avoiding the notorious bottom step, she returned to the basement. "Where are you now?"

"Over here," replied Aunt Susie. "I think these enameled pots were my grandmother's. I can't believe they're still here. I can just see her leaning back from the steam and stirring some of her famous chicken soup. They are pretty banged up, but the bottoms are flat. They would be okay for boiling or steaming or just heating something up. You wouldn't want to fry in them." Aunt Susie didn't even wait for a response; she just tossed them into a box. She continued rifling through crates, muttering, "I bet we'll find some old cast-iron fry pans if we keep looking."

"Let's stop for coffee. I want one of those rolls you made while they're still warm," suggested Jen.

Aunt Susie smiled brightly as she reached to ruffle Jen's auburn hair. She rose, hugged Jen, and headed for the stairs. "Let's go."

Susie took plates from the dish rack and retrieved two still-warm rolls from the cooling rack while Jen grabbed mugs into which she poured the steaming hot java. The two treasured these moments they had alone together. Susie would tell her what life was like when she was younger and occasionally drop some bombshell about Jen's mother's antics when she was a teen—like the time she was caught underage drinking in the local Chinese restaurant by Grandpa's friend, who happened to be a cop. Jen shared almost everything with her aunt and was pretty well convinced that Aunt Susie would never report back to her mother.

"So, Aunt Susie, you never, ever had to move. That is too weird. No getting used to another's idiosyncrasies. No compromising."

"Well, I had to do that plenty with your mom when we were kids. We're three years apart and shared a bedroom for a while. It wasn't until she insisted on sleeping with a night-light and singing herself to sleep that she was moved into the tiny sewing room by our folks." Aunt Susie chuckled, remembering. "We played tea parties with our little china sets, and I always let her serve her Tiny Tears doll first. It wasn't worth my while insisting on having a turn to go first 'cause she would whine to Grandma that I wasn't being fair."

"I didn't know my mom was like that: a whiner as a kid and a rebel as a teenager!"

"Oh, she wasn't bad, just a lot younger than me. So, my wonderful Jen, are you looking forward to having a place of your own?"

"You, bet. Truthfully, it's a little scary knowing that Maggie and I will have to pay for everything ourselves. Living together is a whole lot different from dating, but I don't think we'll have compatibility problems. We've known each other ever since we both had detention for skipping class our sophomore year. I ducked out of chemistry and she out of French. It just took us until we were working adults to realize how we loved each other. Once we get into our first home and have everything all organized, we'll have to put some 'systems into place,' as my dad would say."

"You'll be fine. You know that I'm always here if you need me. That's what aunts are for."

Jen leaped to her feet, leaned over, and gave her aunt a great big hug. "Yup, I know that, and that's why I love you so much. Let's go back and see if we can find those cast-iron pans."

Once back in the basement, the two began searching the final two rooms. There were tightly packed cupboards, boxes on dusty shelves, and old steamer trunks to be examined. The sounds of tearing of paper, creaking of hinges, and thuds of inadvertently dropped items filled the stuffy air.

"You are in luck. Look, here's a ten-inch and a small fry pan. The cast-iron is perfect. No rust or dents. Do you know how to reseason them, or shall I do it for you?"

"If you could, that would be great." Susie climbed over boxes, put the pans on the second to the last step, and made her way to the doorway of the room in which Jen was looking.

"Open those drawers in the Hoosier behind you."

"Hoosier?"

"Yeah, that wooden cupboard with the enamel shelf that pulls out. Have you never seen one? Open the door up top. That's it."

"What the?"

"That's where you stored your flour. When you needed some, you'd push that lever and it came out the chute. If you wanted it sifted, you pressed the lever in and presto, it was all done for you. My grandma had it in her kitchen. I loved being asked to get a cup of flour by my Gran. I would look at her and, thinking I was a clever clogs, would sweetly ask, 'Sifted or plain?' Now open the drawers. I think you'll find some utensils and assorted silverware in there."

Jen did as she was told and stepped back in amazement. The one on the left was filled to the gunnels with assorted knives, spoons, and forks. When she opened the drawer to the right, she found hand utensils of every kind, some for which she didn't know the purpose. "Hey, Aunt Susie. What the heck is this?" she asked as she held up a short red-handled instrument with a wavy blade.

"Oh, that's what my Gran—your great-grandmother—used to cut French fries with. You washed and peeled your potatoes and then cut through one horizontally. Still holding the pieces together, you sliced through the potato the other way. Presto! Potatoes ready to be deep fried. No frozen fries in her day!"

"What a pain!"

"Making French fries was a labor of love for her. She would save all of her used fat in an old can. That was the secret. Boy, were they good!"

"We should go on *Antiques Roadshow* with this stuff."

Susie giggled. "You always find a way to make me laugh. Speaking of road shows, I need to hit the road soon. Throw everything from those drawers into a box and go through them later at your new digs. There are various kitchen things from grandparents, great-grandparents, aunts, and who knows whom else. There may be some useful stuff. I'll grab those old lamps from the other room. You can use them, and when you're flush enough to buy some new ones at IKEA, just pass them on to someone in need or give them to the hospital thrift store."

Aunt Susie and Jen packed the car full, said their good-byes, and then headed off to their respective destinations. As Jen pulled into the driveway of 118 Barlow Lane, she was relieved to see

Maggie's car pulling in behind her. Both girls turned off their engines and bolted out to hug each other.

"So, Mags, how was your first day of being a newly qualified social worker at Elder Services? I'm so proud of you."

"Great, but I'm exhausted. Let's get the deed done."

First, they circled Maggie's car, inspecting the crammed boxes and bags, and then proceeded to do the same at Jen's.

"Did your mother empty her basement into your car like mine did?" queried Maggie.

"No, it was my Aunt Susie's doing. Look at our cars! I think we'll have to do some culling of the junk. Let's empty my car first, and then we can reverse cars and do yours."

"Great idea. It'll save us a few steps—which we will appreciate, considering we need to hike up to the top floor. Energy will be saved for the unpacking"

It took nearly an hour and a half to drag the acquired necessities of a first abode to the second-floor apartment. There were bags, boxes, lamps, end tables, and who knows what else everywhere in the four rooms of the apartment.

Jen raised her hands above her head and waved them about. "Where do we even begin?"

"I work much better on a full stomach. Let's order some Chinese, and while we're waiting, we can clear an eating space in the kitchen and begin putting things away."

"Great idea, Mags. You're always the voice of reason in our capers. Here, let's order on the iPad." Once the girls selected tasty delights, they entered the necessary info to ensure delivery in thirty minutes.

Jen grabbed the box containing the unused bank dinnerware and gave it all a rinse before leaving it to drain in the rack. She began looking for her box of silverware when Maggie produced the bag of cutlery donated by her grandmother. She dumped it into the sink of sudsy water with a splash that managed to wet Jen, who was just lifting her sought-after box.

"Maggie, you have almost as much of a mishmash there as I do. When you finish, I'll plunk mine in. I didn't look at it when I was at my aunt's, I just took it. I bet it will need rinsing too."

"All set. I'm drying now."

Both girls were soaked by the splashing created as Jen emptied the contents of the Hoosier's drawers into the soapy water. That led to a long and hilarious bubbles fight that was abruptly ended by a ringing doorbell and both women covered from head to toe in foam. Jen answered the door, gave the deliveryman a generous tip, and brought the food to the table. Maggie grabbed plates and reached for serving spoons from her stash.

They dove into the crab rangoons—using their hands, as any red-blooded American would do—and voraciously devoured every last bit. When they moved on to the rice and chicken, they scooped out the food with the serving spoons Maggie had retrieved.

"Damn," Jen bleeped as the spoon from the rice slipped out of her hand and clattered to the floor. "Oh, no worries. I'll grab one from my bowl of stuff." She reached into the soapy water, grabbed a handle, and gave the spoon a good rinse and dry. She settled back onto her chair and helped herself to rice.

Maggie looked surprised. "Hey, I thought you were getting one of your spoons. What did you do? Wash mine?"

"No, I got this one from the sink. Yours is still on the floor." Jen pointed to the simply engraved spoon still lying where it had fallen.

Both girls stared at it and then at the one in Jen's hand. Maggie scooted to the floor, grabbed her spoon, and returned to her place.

"Look! Look! They match, they match. They both have those tiny roses on the bowls. We have the same spoon. Now that's weird. How could that happen? I found mine in my grandmother's basement. How about you?"

"Mine came from a drawer in a Hoosier thingy that belonged to my great-grandmother. It was in Aunt Susie's cellar."

"In a what?"

"Hoosier—it's an old-fashioned kitchen type of cupboard. Why do you think we both showed up with identical spoons?" Jen wondered.

"Kind of like *The Twilight Zone*, don't you think?"

Jen continued, "Seriously, do you think it's a coincidence, or is there a reason for both of our relatives to have had the same spoon?"

"Who knows? Maybe the spoons were a freebie at some time, like the dishes from the bank that your aunt had."

"But that means someone from my family and someone from yours must have . . ." persisted Jen.

While pondering the possibilities of such a serendipitous event, the doorbell rang again. "I just don't get it, do you?" asked Maggie as she opened the door to a smiling Aunt Susie, whose arms were filled with a plant and a bottle of chilled Prosecco to toast the new home.

"You don't get what?" asked the favorite aunt.

"Come see this." Maggie led her to the table, where she put down the wine and flowers. "Look! We both brought the same serving spoon."

"Yeah, Aunt Susie. Look. This came from your grandmother's Hoosier, and this one came from Maggie's grandmother's basement. Isn't that weird?"

Susie plopped onto a chair and picked up a spoon in each hand. She carefully inspected the spoons and measured the width of the bowl with her fingers. She looked up at her niece and her partner and shook her head before flipping the spoons over to further examine the back.

"This is going to require some sleuthing, don't you think? I know my grandmother used this spoon . . . no, this one . . . well, one of these spoons on special occasions. She always would smile when she took it out and then would polish it lovingly with her apron. I can see her doing it right now. She once told me it was unusual to have engravings on the bowl of a spoon. Maggie, what do you know about yours?"

"Nothing! My grandmother just gave me a box of stuff and said 'take it.'"

Susie continued to examine the spoons while the girls resumed stuffing their faces. She put them down gingerly and spied glasses sitting on the counter. Although they were juice glasses, she rinsed and dried three of them and brought them back to the table. She popped the cork of the Prosecco, poured a healthy splash into each glass, and announced, "A toast."

The girls beamed and lifted their glasses, waiting for Susie's words.

"Here's to two wonderful women starting a new life together in their own apartment, and to solving the mystery of two spoons. Cheers!"

"Cheers!" chimed the happy couple.

That night, Maggie tossed and turned. She couldn't shake the feeling that the matching spoons could be very significant. But why? What possible reason could there be for her grandmother and Jen's great-grandmother to have such rare matching spoons. Did it really matter? When the first rays of light filtered through the blinds, Maggie carefully slipped out of bed so as not to wake Jen. She put on her robe and slid her feet into her slippers before padding into the kitchen.

Maggie filled the kettle, pressed the START button, and reached for a teabag and mug. She glanced at the microwave clock and saw that it was just past seven; Gran would be on her second cup of coffee by now. When the water boiled, she poured it over the bag and left it to steep while she called her grandmother.

"Good morning, favorite granddaughter. You're up early."

"Hi, Gran. I couldn't sleep. I'm so excited to be setting up a home with Jen. I have to ask you, where did all the stuff come from that you gave me?"

"Oh, my dear. From various people. I'm just a collector of things that people want to throw away. I live what my mother always preached: 'Waste not, and want not.'"

"But do you remember who gave you what? I'm especially curious about a silver serving spoon engraved on the bowl, of all places, with a simple but pretty rose."

"Oh, my dear, I'm not sure I remember exactly. Most of the old stuff came from my mother or my aunt, her older sister. I didn't have things from her younger sister because she died of TB at a young age."

"I didn't know I had great-aunts. Can we come to visit, and will you tell me more about them?"

"Of course! That will motivate me to turn those overripe bananas into bread. Will it be for morning coffee or afternoon tea?"

Maggie laughed. "We'll be there about eleven so the banana bread will still be warm. Love you, Gran. See you later."

As Maggie hung up the phone, a very drowsy Jen slipped into the kitchen, rubbing her eyes. "What's up? Who you talking to so early? Morning." She bent over and placed a kiss on Maggie's forehead and smiled.

"My Gran. I couldn't get those damn spoons out of my head all night. I wanted to solve the mystery of the matching spoons and see if I could find out from where my spoon came. Gran invited us for coffee, and she's making banana bread to go with it. I told her we'd be there around eleven."

Jen laughed as she responded, "Between them, they keep us well fed. Your grandmother makes banana bread, and my Aunt Susie does the cinnamon rolls. Maybe they are secretly related."

After emptying yet more boxes and showering, they headed out in plenty of time to stop at Just Blooming to buy flowers for Maggie's grandmother. "I don't know why, but my Gran loves daisies. I always have the florist stick a few in bouquets to make her happy." Maggie smiled as she showed the fragrant flowers to Jen.

The girls had barely shut the car doors before Gran was at the top steps of her porch, wearing, as always, an apron to protect her clothes. She was drying her hands on a towel that was neatly tucked into her waistband. "You two have made my day. I love your company! Come here and give me a hug."

The girls smothered Gran with hugs and kisses and followed her into the tidy kitchen. The aroma of freshly baked banana bread filled the room, and a flick of a switch set the coffeemaker to work.

"Here you go, Gran. Flowers for the best grandmother on the planet."

"Oh, that's because I have the best granddaughter. Thank you. They're beautiful and you always remember the daisies. I'll set them into a pitcher for a good long drink of water and arrange them later."

Once the flowers were safe, Gran indicated that they were all to take a seat around the well-used tin-topped table. "Now tell me all about your first apartment. Is it cozy? Do you need anything else?"

"Oh, it's lovely," replied Maggie. "And as soon as it's not a hazard for you to walk through the place, we'll have you for dinner. We still don't know what we need because we both brought loads of stuff and haven't finished unpacking. But something very crazy happened. It's kind of a puzzle, and we thought you may help us find some answers."

"Well, I can sure try. What do you need to know?"

"Where did all of the kitchen stuff that you gave me come from?"

"Oh, I don't know exactly. Some was my mother's, and some was probably from your grandpa's family. There may have been a few items from my aunt, and of course, some it was mine from when I was first married."

Jen could restrain herself no longer. She took a spoon out of her shoulder bag and handed it across the table. "Does this look familiar?"

Gran reached for the spoon and drew it toward her. She examined it closely, turning it over and over in her hand. "Isn't it pretty? The size and the weight of it make it rest perfectly in your hand, and look at the beautiful little rose on the bowl. I just don't remember it at all. Was there only one like it?"

"As a matter of fact, no," replied Maggie. "Here's a matching one. But this is the mystery: it came from Jen's Aunt Susie's basement."

Gran reached for the second spoon and compared the two. The girls could sense that she was trying to work it all out as she carefully examined both spoons. She shook her head slowly from side to side. "Too bad my Aunt Babs isn't still with us. She loved a good mystery."

"Who is this Aunt Babs, Gran? I never knew your mother had sisters until you mentioned it on the phone this morning."

"Oh, she was kind of the black sheep in the family. Mother was forbidden to talk about her by my dad. You see, it was scandalous in those days for two women to love one another. All I know is that Aunt Babs moved in with a beautiful lady, the daughter of someone very influential in their town. They set up a home like newlyweds, money was never an issue. Mother said it didn't take long for people to gossip about things that shouldn't have concerned them, and Babs's lover was dragged away by her powerful family."

"Oh my god. That's horrible. My god, what happened to Babs?"

"Heartbroken. After a few months, she moved to a West Coast city. She worked and became a very successful businesswoman. She stayed in contact for a few years, especially around the holidays. Then, when I was about twelve, my mother received a letter and a box in the mail from a lawyer stating Aunt Babs had died. She had bequeathed most of her estate to various charities that helped destitute women and/or children, but for the few items in the box that was to be sent to her only sister. Your great-grandmother was her only next of kin."

"Gran, why did I never hear about her? She couldn't be with her family? That's so tragic! I don't understand. After all, I have Jen, and all of you guys love her."

"Maggie and Jen, times were different then, and even up to just a few years ago. I'm so grateful that you two will have an easier time of it," she said and gently smiled. "Maybe that spoon came from Aunt Babs's box. Who knows?"

"That would be awesome," chimed in Jen.

The three women chatted about every day things as they finished their coffee and warm banana bread that was baked with love.

Jen gathered the plates and mugs and washed them. Spying the flowers, she asked, "Can I arrange these for you?"

"No, thank you, my dear. I like doing it, and it'll give me a project to do after you girls leave. Now, off you go. I'm sure there's plenty for you to do to make your new apartment a home."

With that small hint that Gran was ready to be left on her own, the girls bade farewell with hugs and kisses and headed for the car. They were both quiet as Jen backed out to the street.

"So, Jen, what do you think? My great-aunt was a lesbian. Who would have guessed?"

"What do I think? I think we better drop in on my aunt and find out a little bit more about her grandmother who always smiled when she saw her spoon," suggested Jen.

They exchanged meaningful looks.

"What a plan! Let's go now. Do you think you should call her first?"

"No, it's Aunt Susie. It'll be fine." With that, Jen used a driveway to turn around in order to get to her aunt's house more quickly. It was a silent fifteen-minute ride, with both women lost in their individual thoughts.

Jen rapped on the door loudly and, as usual, walked right in. "Aunt Susie, Aunt Susie," she called as she made her way from the kitchen into the dining room She looked lovingly at the old formal table and buffet. "This is where we had all our family holidays as long as I can remember," she told Maggie. "Aunt Susie, where are you?"

"Here, in the den. I didn't expect to see you so soon. What's the panic?"

Maggie and Jen reached the den and saw the beloved aunt comfortably settled in the overstuffed chair by the bow window, knitting away on a new project. Kisses and greetings exchanged, the girls seated themselves near her on the sofa.

Jen began, "We're trying to figure out the spoons. Well, really, Maggie began and I just jumped on the bandwagon." They exchanged a smile of acknowledgment.

"So tell me—tell me what you've found out," demanded Susie.

"We think my spoon came from a great-aunt I didn't even know I had," jumped in Maggie.

"So, can you tell us something about your grandmother—meaning my great-grandmother, Aunt Susie?"

"What do you want to know?"

Jen explained, "Last night, you said she only brought the spoon out on special occasions. You said she would polish it carefully and look at it lovingly. Tell us more about that. Try and remember. Did she ever tell you where it came from?"

"Oh, Jen. She would look at it as if it were her biggest treasure. The corners of her lips would turn up, her eyes would brighten, and she'd give her head a little shake. I did once ask her where she got it."

"What did she say? What did she say?" interrupted Jen.

"She said something about it coming from a very long time ago. When I asked if it had been a wedding gift, she said something so mysterious that I remember her exact words. She said, 'No, before that. A time most people have forgotten, but probably when my heart was its happiest. A time when the world did not understand, but my dear friend and I did.'"

"Whoa, Aunt Susie. Did you ask her to explain?"

"She wouldn't say any more about it. She said someday I would figure things out, but I never did."

Jen persisted. "Did you ask your mother?"

Aunt Susie laughed and reached forward to touch Jen's cheek. "You know how you and I share things that you and your mother don't? Well, my Gran and I were like that. I am not sure my mother even noticed. When I asked her about it, she looked at me as if I were from outer space and said she did not have a clue about the spoon and knew little of Gran's life between school and marriage."

There was a brief silence, and then Jen and Maggie exchanged glances.

"What's going on?" asked a perplexed aunt.

"We think we can tell you about my great-grandmother's secret," replied Jen.

They took out the matching spoons from their pockets, clanked them together, and began.

By the Light of an October Moon

As Kate started to draw the bedroom drapes, she glanced out the window. Nights like these were made for fitful sleeping. The autumn moon cast an eerie glow, the kind that should be in a film like *The Legend of Sleepy Hollow*. Without turning to look at him, she remarked, "Bill, look at how the full moon is causing the frost on the green to glisten. Bill . . ."

She turned to look at her husband of more years than most couples had managed to achieve. He was sawing wood again in very deep rhythmic tones. She shook her head from side to side and let out a long audible sigh. She grabbed her robe and picked up the china cup and saucer that held her carefully prepared chamomile tea with honey, gently stirred it with the ancient family teaspoon, and headed down the stairs to get a better look at the moonlit green from her front door.

She was so grateful that they had decided to buy this antique house, despite having to live austerely and to use the entire upstairs of rambling rooms as a seasonal bed-and-breakfast to finance it. The village green had so much charm, surrounded by the houses of whaling captains and a few historical churches. Rumor had it that a few of the houses were underground railway stations, and some believed the spirits of the departed occasionally put in an appearance. Many ghost hunters had stayed as guests in their inn, which was furnished in such a manner that one would think that it was the 1700s when Benjamin Sanford had built it, albeit electronics. They always remained awake in the reception rooms throughout the night, hoping to see a vision of anyone from the past, and crashed during the day, making it hard to get the rooms cleaned. Some were disappointed; others claimed to have witnessed the spirit of Benjamin Sanford himself. Maybe someday the rest of the family will feel as connected to the remarkable house and green as she does. Now they just think of it as a dinosaur that required too much work to maintain.

As she opened the door, the nearly 250-year-old bell in the white clapboard Congregational church across the village green began ringing. *Dong! Dong! Dong!* She shook her head in disbelief as the bell never rang at night. Bending down, she stretched her neck upward to see who was pulling the rope. *Dong! Dong! Dong!*

Kate stepped outside to get a better look when a *Ding! Ding! Ding!* began to chime from the stone Episcopal church three doors down from her house. "What the heck?" she cried out loud. Still holding the cup and saucer, which once belonged to her grandmother, she gingerly stepped down the stoop so as not to slip and continued along the icy path while stirring in the honey.

Dong! Dong! Dong! And then came the reply: *Ding! Ding!*

Kate silently opened the gate, checked the deserted street, crossed over the road, and ducked under the white split rail fence that surrounded the village green. Mystified by the ringing of one bell and the response of the other, she turned her attention from church steeple to church steeple. When the ringing ended, she inched her way to the middle of the triangular-shaped green so she could easily see both churches at the same time. Unsure as to whether she had imagined the midnight peal of bells, she shook her head and began to make her way back home. She pulled the collar of her fleece robe up to protect her neck from the frosty autumnal evening, tightened the belt, and turned for one last look. Something glimmered in her peripheral vision. A shimmering light spilled down from the belfry of the stone church and hit the ground where she had been standing just a few seconds ago. It was like a spotlight, only very dim.

She stood ramrod straight but was quickly distracted by a similar light streaming from the steeple of the wooden church. The two light beams floated through the air and danced around each other before intertwining. When two diffuse figures formed from the light, Kate gasped and leaned against the fence.

A tall, slender, spectral man wearing a tricorn hat, britches, waistcoat, and riding boots grasped the hands of an equally faint man dressed in a rather weather-beaten ship officer's uniform of days gone past, complete with a brimmed hat. He sported a long white, neatly shaped beard and muttonchops. They chatted animatedly but in such quiet voices, Kate could not make out the words they exchanged. Laughter and slaps on the back showed the ease between them. The younger man produced a mug of ale with a snap of his fingers, and the bearded man snapped his fingers and received a jigger of what appeared, from the rising steam, to be hot rum.

Kate stared, her mouth hanging open, and slipped to the ground. Although she had made no sound, the men were startled, looked her way, and acknowledged her presence as they both nodded their heads. She responded with the slightest flick of a hand. They continued with their conversation, occasionally looking her way.

"Oh my god. Am I dreaming? Hallucinating?" Kate put her cup and saucer down and purposely hit herself with the silver teaspoon to see if she was conscious. "Ouch! Yup, I'm here all right!"

The night seemed to take on a deeper chill, and Kate huddled into a ball to limit the surface area exposed to the late autumnal air as she watched the apparently old friends in animated conversation. *What could they possibly be talking about?* she wondered. Eventually, the old salt nudged his chum. He looked in her direction, stood up, and called ever so softly, "Come here. Let us help you."

Kate shook her head no and pulled in tightly.

"We won't harm you," he replied.

She could not control her body as she was gently levitated to where the men had sat themselves. Kate raised the hand that was still grasping the teaspoon tightly and waved hello. The younger man broke into a broad smile and reached out and tapped the spoon. Kate reacted by stuffing it into the pocket of her blue candlewick robe.

"I thought that looked familiar. It came from a special order I filled in my shop years back. Each piece of cutlery had a tiny little rose engraved in the bowl. It wasn't as easy to do as I thought it would be. As usual, I stuck to my originally stated fee for the set, so the family certainly must have been pleased with such a bargain."

Kate pulled the spoon from her pocket and studied it. There was indeed a tiny rose on it, and she glanced from the spoon to the man with her mouth hanging open. He did have a familiar face, but she was unable to speak, so she silently put it back in the safety of her pocket.

The snowy-haired man interrupted him. "Here, my dear. Take my old coat. It is tattered but warm. Your lips are turning blue, and you're shivering so loudly I can hear your teeth chatter, even at my age."

Before Kate could object, the coat floated onto her shoulders. She nodded in disbelief but appreciated the gesture.

"Now have a tot of rum to warm your insides."

A glass of hot buttered rum with steam still rising dropped into her hand, and uncontrollably, she lifted it to her lips and sipped the warming liquor. It seemed hours had passed as the men continued chatting, and Kate kept listening. They talked about many things: courage, freedom, friends lost, battles won, and upcoming elections that had actually happened centuries ago. They spoke of metalwork, seamanship, taxes, and the costs of liberty.

"Well, Paul, it's a shame we cannot align here more than a few hours on this particular full moon each year. I would love a good game of cribbage with you."

"I'll bring a board next year. But, my friend, perhaps we need to play whist instead so our new friend here could join in the fun." He smiled.

Kate's eyes widened and she gasped. "Oh yes, please. Oh, and thank you for the bell that still rings in that church across the green. Folks love knowing it was made by you."

"My foundry sure knew how to make them so they'd last." The man smiled, turning toward the steeple.

"So next October's full moon, just listen for my bell," replied the younger man.

"The bells of my descendants' house of worship too," added the other man with a smile.

The coat floated from Kate's shoulders onto the arm of the kindly man to whom it belonged. "I'll bring the rum and the playing cards. The cloak too, in case you're chilly." He broke into a smile and reached out to touch Kate's cheek as gently as her father would have done.

Both men got to their feet, tipped their hats toward her, and shook hands before dissolving into one light. The beam swirled about and then separated into two distinct rays. One swept to the stone church, and the other retreated to the white clapboard church. There was a flash from each tower, and Kate scrambled to her feet as she heard the *Dong! Dong! Dong!* distinctly followed by a *Ding! Ding!*

Kate picked up the cup and saucer, ran for her front door, and put it on the top stone step so she could throw the old heavy door open. She retrieved it and practically fell into the hallway before slamming the door shut. She left the china on the hall table and ran up the stairs with the shot glass that still held the remains of the rum in her hand. She screamed, "Bill! Bill! You won't believe this . . ."

Good old Bill! There he was, still sawing logs and shaking the whole house, as usual. She shook her head, put the glass on her nightstand, removed her robe, and pulled back the sheets on her side of the bed. As she cuddled under the duvet, she whispered, "Forget it. You would never believe me anyhow."

Kate tossed and turned for what seemed like hours, so she was completely surprised when Bill crept into the bedroom, opened the drapes, and presented her with a steaming mug of freshly brewed coffee and the morning paper. As she rose to a sitting position, she shook her head, trying to make out whether she had dreamed what was in her thoughts or actually lived it.

"Morning, Kate. You were sleeping soundly when I got up to let the cat out. You didn't appear after an hour, so I thought you'd want me to wake you before your yoga class. It's at ten, right?"

"Yes, you're a dear. Hey, last night, did you . . ."

Bill glanced down as he placed the mug of java on the night table. First, the color drained from his face; then he turned beet red before he interrupted his wife. "How did you get my glass?" demanded Bill. He reached for the rum glass that Kate had put on the bottom shelf of her nightstand.

"Yours? Yours? What are you talking about? That's mine!" she snapped as she grabbed it back.

"Where did you get it? I had it tucked deep into the pocket of the L. L. Bean fleece you gave me for my birthday. Have you been snooping around my clothes?"

Bill was furious. Every inch of his face was bright red, and he was clenching his teeth while pacing about the bedroom. The floorboards creaked as he went about his tantrum. Kate had never seen him like this in their thirty-five years of marriage.

"Bill, that's mine! A friend gave it to me just . . . just recently. And why would you hide a glass in the pocket of a winter garment at the back of your closet, anyways?"

"Oh yeah? And who would that mysterious person be?" he retorted.

"Wait, Bill. If you think this is yours from the fleece, go and see if it is missing from there."

"Sure, I'd be happy to prove you took it."

Bill stomped to his closet and threw open the creaky door. He pushed several hangers of clothes out of his way and finally came to the fleece that was in the middle of his winter apparel. He lifted the hanger off the railing and tossed it to Kate.

"Here you go, madam. Check my pockets!"

Kate shook her head, put her glass on the nightstand next to the cooling coffee, took in a deep breath, and let it out loudly to show her annoyance. She looked down and reached into the right side pocket of the fleece. Nothing. She turned the garment around and thrust her hand into the other pocket and broke into a smile. Slowly, she withdrew an object wrapped in a cotton handkerchief.

Kate looked at Bill with raised eyebrows and handed it over. Bill looked shocked. He slowly removed a small glass that surely still gave off a fragrance of rum from the old hankie. He held it up high, looked confused, and walked over to Kate's side of the bed. She took the glass from him and carefully examined it. As she was doing so, he reached for the glass Kate had placed on her nightstand and began examining it. Their eyes met, each showing a bit of unease, and slowly they held the glasses side by side.

"They match perfectly. Bill, where did you get your glass? And when did you start drinking rum instead of Miller Lite?"

"A friend gave it to me. That's when I drank a little hot buttered rum."

"Did your friend happen to wear clothes that seemed a little out of date?"

"Yes, did yours?"

Kate patted the other side of the bed. Bill moved around, kicked off his slippers, and settled down next to his wife.

"I think we better have a little chat, don't you?"

THE INTERVIEW

"Oh, hello. Do come in. You're from the radio station, right?"

"Okay. Come sit in the parlor."

"Would you like a cup of tea? I just brewed a pot."

"No? Are you sure? You'll be missing out on some good brew. Have a seat here—it's the best chair."

"This spoon? My mama's . . . isn't the rose here on the bowl pretty? My daddy bought it for her because her name was Rose. Now is that microphone on? Are you taping this? Do they still call it taping?"

"Oh, okay. Now what is it that you want to know? Where do you want me to start?"

"I'm Irene McKay, and I've been resident here in this town of Fulton for all ninety-nine years of my life. That's good 'cause with this macular degeneration, I can't see so well, but I remember how to get where I need to go. I've good neighbors who drive me if I can't walk to where I need to be. I never wanted to leave here, but my folks made me accept that scholarship to Wellesley College. Spent four years outside of Boston studying the fine arts and then scurried right back here to this town."

"Oh, I'm just not a city girl. I need to smell the ocean breezes and hear the sounds of the waves. I like to mark the seasons by the sounds of the birds and insects and what fresh fish and veggies are in the market. I need to know the people who are walking down the street, picking up my trash, and delivering my mail. I want to know if the stranger sitting in the coffee shop is here with good intentions or evil ones. I know that some people call me the village busybody, but I'm not at all. I just want to make sure that Fulton remains the idyllic New England town for everyone, today and in the future, because one bad patch for all of us here in Fulton was enough."

"No, my family's all gone now, so there's just me. I was an only child. My husband—God bless him—died in a horrible accident. He was trying to rescue the Jones boy the day he fell through the ice on the pond behind the school. Unfortunately, they both went into the water, and it was so cold that day that the ice froze right over before he could get the boy out. Our only son, Matthew, moved to the West Coast after high school to become a movie star. The only star he became was one in the sky after he overdosed on something or other. So the people of this town became my family, and many still help me out so I can stay right here in the family homestead instead of one of those ghastly senior-citizen homes. Yup, I pretty much know everyone and, I hasten to add, everyone in Fulton probably knows me."

"Oh yes. I remember a lot of things others have forgotten. Janey—the lady at the Fulton Historical Society—keeps nagging me to write down everything I know about the people and the town. Why, that would take me another ninety-nine years. There's just so much to tell, and of course, I have all the diaries and scrapbooks my mother kept as well. Between us, we would total about 140 years to talk about."

"Oh, sorry, I do ramble at times. You want to hear about something that no one else knows about except me? Let's see. I wonder what would be of the most interest to you. Hmmm.

There are loads of stories from the War of 1812, but that was way before my time. Of course, there were loads of servicemen stationed here during World War II. Did you know this town was a staging post for the Americal Division before they shipped out to the Pacific? The USO building used to be where the recreation center is now. There was always something going on there, and lots of us girls would go there to serve coffee or dance with the lonely men. Some of them were really just boys pretending to be men."

"I remember that one Valentine's Day, the USO wanted to organize an evening the boys would never forget. Some of us girls never forgot it either, but I am the only one still alive to tell you about it. First, there was buffet supper. They had all kinds of sliced meats and salads. To start, there was clam chowder. New England style, of course—we don't abide by that red stuff here. We ladies just helped ourselves and sat down at tables, leaving empty chairs between each of us. That way, every soldier would have a girl to talk to when the men were finally invited to help themselves and take a seat. Oh, we all ate, laughed, and had a good time. Soon the band started playing, and the dancing began. Before I could blink, I had a full dance card, but I was enamored of a young airman named Charles."

"Don't recall his last name, but oh, he was so handsome. Tall, dark curly hair, and clean-shaven. I never did abide a man with facial hair. I 'accidentally' tossed out my card and spent the whole evening dancing with him. He smiled and chatted about his mama and described his hometown. He made me laugh easily with the little jokes he made about the couples around us. At times, he seemed a bit distracted and was making gestures to a friend of his across the room, who was leaning against the wall near the door. After a bit, he asked me if I would do him a favor. He wanted me to hold on to a key until he came back from overseas. He'd come and get it then. I thought, *why me?* He didn't know me from Adam, but my father always said we should do whatever we could to give these poor boys who were being shipped out some peace of mind. If tucking a key away in some secret place was going to make him feel at ease before shipping out to war—well, I could do that."

"So I said 'Yes, how will you find me?'"

He replied, "No matter how long it takes, no matter where you are, I—or someone in my behalf—will find you."

"Now, being a foolish nineteen-year-old, I thought that very mysterious and quite romantic. But now I wonder."

"Oh, I am off track, sorry. At that point, he handed me the key, kissed me good-bye, and left with his friend. I put it in the little pocket of my clutch purse, which was meant to hold a mirror. I had broken mine, and the key fit in it perfectly."

"No, I neither heard from him nor his friends."

"No, I didn't think to ask what the key opened. It was his, and it didn't occur to me to ask. I wonder though . . ."

"Oh yes, back to other happenings in town. Let's see. I'm pretty sure the dance was a few days after the night I was awoken by blaring sirens and clanging alarms. Somehow all the three banks in town were robbed at the same time that night. The police weren't even sure if all were burgled by the same group of hoodlums or if it was an amazing coincidence. That was way before alarms did anything other than clang loudly, so no photos or text messages to the police station like today. All together, five million in cash and stashes of sterling silver, gold, platinum, and jewels were heisted from the banks but never recovered. No clues, no suspects. You never ever hear anyone talk about that robbery now. Maybe it's a cold case. I don't remember reading that it was solved. I wonder if all of that bounty was hidden away somewhere or if it was all spent. Hey, maybe I hold the key. Now that would be funny!"

"What? It's been eighty years, and you want what? That's no microphone, is it?"

REST MY SOUL

Wow, it's a palindrome. That's too weird. I wonder how many times a digital clock would read the same forwards and backwards in one day. I'll have to make that the problem of the week in class on Monday.

I threw off the comforter and guided my feet into slippers to make my nightly bathroom trip, but the numbers bothered me. I knew there was something special about 3:33 but couldn't remember what I had heard or where I had heard it. I rid myself of the few beers I had enjoyed at Trivia Night at Liam's and started trotting back to bed. Why was Alan, my curmudgeon of a teenager, calling me?

I headed back to his room and stuck my head in to see what the problem was. He was sound asleep. His legs stuck out from the end of the bed, and one arm nearly touched the floor. His comforter barely reached his waist so, being a mother, I snuck in and rearranged his bedding so he was all covered. And I placed a kiss on the crown of his head. He didn't move a muscle.

Back in the sack, I snuggled under my goose down comforter. My room seemed colder than when I left to pee. I cocooned into the comforts and familiar smells of the freshly laundered sheets and began to drift off when I heard Alan calling me once again. *What's going on? Did he take something illegal?* Off went my sheets, and as I angrily stomped toward the door, the air felt even chillier. Suddenly, the door slammed shut with a bang. I jumped back in surprise as it was such a still night there wasn't even the slightest breeze.

"Come here! Come here!" squeaked a weak, raspy voice. I turned toward the sound but could see nothing. Maybe I took something of Alan's without knowing it. "Here, over here," it pleaded more earnestly. "Here, come here."

Trancelike, I followed the sound until the voice slowly became loud enough for me to hear the words distinctly. I was drawn around the end of the bed and up the other side. My eyes darted from here to there in search of the voice until, finally, I saw a soft, muted light emanating from behind the night table. Gingerly, I lifted the table, placed it at the foot of the bed, and squatted down to get a better look. There seemed to be wisps of color in the diffuse light. I could only stare in wonder at this illumination. Slowly the colors swirled, all blending together at first and then separating to form the image of a tiny man.

I froze in place, but the sweat poured down my face. The handsome muscular man tipped his hat and slowly smiled at me. He was dressed in worn pants that were gathered at the knees and held up by braided hemp tied into a knot. His faded plaid shirt was collarless and unbuttoned at the top, and he was barefoot. His feet were scarred and his hands calloused from years of hard work. "I found you at last. God is good," he whispered.

"Me? You found me? How do you know? Who do you think I am, and who or what are you? Why—"

"Doesn't matter who I am as long as you are Lizbeth Coulter, and I know that is you. I have been wandering, a lost spirit, for more than 150 years. I can't join my beloved beyond God's Gate until I've finished one piece of business, and you can help me on my way. Please, Ms. Coulter, help me be free of the good Earth so I can leave behind the memories, which are truly the remaining shackles of slavery."

"Oh boy, I must've either had way too much to drink or someone slipped something into my beer. I'm hallucinating and talking to light beams. Alan! Alan! Get in here!"

"Shhhhhh! Ma'am, please. Just you and me. Don't be afraid. I've never knowingly hurt anyone with my hands or words and surely will not hurt you as you're my key to heaven. Sit down here next to me and I'll explain."

Slowly I slipped to the floor, totally mesmerized by who or what was in front of me. I stretched out my right hand toward the diffuse light, and the tiny figure climbed onto the back of it. I could feel nothing except strange warmth where the tiny feet touched my skin. Carefully I moved my hand upward so my eyes would be level with his eyes. They were soft, gentle eyes—eyes that showed pain and love at the same time. A sense of calm and trust spread through me, and I gingerly rose, climbed onto my bed while balancing my guest on my right hand, and pulled the covers over me with my left. He jumped onto my chest, and when I sat up, supported by pillows, our eyes were once again level.

He took a deep breath and began to talk. "Way back in the sixties—the 1860s—I was the property of Master Byron Wright. His name may be *Wright*, but he surely was not! He sold my wife, Sunny, to a man with whom he had a big gambling debt."

"Sold her? What are you talking about?" I asked, trying to comprehend what I was hearing.

The little man raised his hand, silencing me. "Ma'am, we were his property, and he could do as he pleased. We had no say. I begged that he not sell Sunny because I loved her more than anyone could love another person, and I didn't know what kind of a master the new one would be. 'Sell me instead,' I pleaded. He just laughed and said that Sunny could produce some good strong bucks, so she was worth a bundle, and off she went."

"Oh my god! How heartless! How inhumane!"

"My broken heart told me what to do. Run away, find Sunny, and head North. I waited until we had a spell of hot, dry days so I would leave no tracks and then made my way by the silver light of the moon. I traveled by night and hid from slave catchers during the day. I crossed streams, creeks, and ponds so my scent would be left behind."

"Where did you sleep? How were you able to stay safe?"

He shook his head and continued, "Must've been on the run near a fortnight when I came upon a small house set back from the dirt road. Dawn would soon be upon me, but I noticed that the missus had left some laundry on the line—must've been wet. I passed by and turned in my tracks. There was a colorful quilt stitched with beautiful stars, and in the middle, I swear I saw the drinking gourd. Hesitantly, I returned, murmured a quick and silent prayer, and crept up to the cabin. Holding my breath, I rapped gently on the door and stood silently. The gingham curtains were parted, and the bolts slipped open."

"Weren't you frightened? How did you know it was safe there?"

He nodded appreciatively. "I was greeted with a sweet smile and fed a hearty bowl of chicken stew with slabs of bread and butter. Was it ever tasty! When I had finished the last morsel, the mistress walked out over the property and into the barn to make sure I was not followed. When she was convinced it was safe, she beckoned me to join her in the barn."

"Why? Why didn't she just give you a bed in her cabin?"

"She needed to stay safe for the sake of those who would follow me. Behind the stacks of straw were several small doors leading into coops for chicken, geese, and ducks. One little door secretly led to a snug little hidey-hole of a coop where I was to spend the day that was dawning. Mrs. Coulter reached into the deep pocket of her apron and pulled out something wrapped in a forest-green linen napkin. 'Sell this if you need money along your way. Be careful, my son, and may God bless and protect you,' she said to me."

"What a courageous woman. I wish I'd known her. How long did she hide you?"

He continued, "When the sun had gone to bed, I stole away under the protective cover of darkness provided by the good Lord. I traveled safely by night for two days, and then my luck ran out. I was nabbed from behind a holly bush by a couple of bounty hunters. They knocked me about and gagged me with a strip of burlap sacking before shackling my ankles. While they were busy making sure I'd never escape, I managed to slip that green napkin down my pant leg. I have no idea what they were paid by my master for bringing me back, but they sure were happy."

"They were paid for capturing you? They should've had their hands cut off!"

"They didn't even hang around long enough to see the master tell Mr. Laurence, the overseer, to give me one hundred lashes for trying to escape. He needed to make an example of me. Every inch of me ached or burned, but I wouldn't give Mr. Laurence the satisfaction of seeing a tear or hearing me cry. That night, Momma May took me to her quarters, cleaned up my back, and wrapped me in salve-laden gauze. She sang to me in soothing tones, asking the Lord to care for me until I fell into a deep sleep."

"Were you able to rest until your wounds had healed?" I asked naively.

He smiled at me sweetly but shook his head no. "The very next day, I was back in the fields, working in the sun, and planning my next attempt to find Sunny. I was angry but still determined to find her. Days went by, but I was still planning. The good Lord must've been listening in on me and the rest of my people because news spread like fire that the war was done and President Lincoln had freed us all."

He shut his eyes, and he seemed totally lost in thought. I waited reverently until he was ready to continue his story. Slowly he looked at me again, and his sweet smile broadened.

"Great shouts of 'Praise the Lord' rang out, and our people were dancing and singing. It was such a joyful time."

"Oh, thank God you were saved. But what about your Sunny? Where was she?"

"First thing I did was set out to find my Sunny. Her former mistress had taken a shining to her, and as the master had passed, she offered us a few acres to sharecrop. We had no place to go, no plans, so that was where we set up our home and raised our children. Some times were good and others pretty rough, especially when the rain wouldn't come. We were pretty happy except the year of the big drought. Sunny begged me to unwrap whatever was in that napkin to help us get through these bad times. That was the only time I ever said no to that woman."

"But why? It could've helped your family," I insisted.

"It wasn't ours to use. It belonged to Mistress Coulter. It was to be used to buy freedom, and Mr. Lincoln gave that to us all. It has to be returned. When Sunny passed, I left my children in the care of Sister Aimee and retraced my old steps to do just that, return the wrapped treasure. After a few weeks, I found where the Coulter house used to stand, but all that was left was the foundation, chimney, and root cellar. It had been burned to the ground, and there were no signs of that gentle, brave lady. Feeling like a failure, I returned to my children, and I saw them grow into adults, marry, and bring me grandbabies. When my body left Earth, my youngest daughter remembered the green napkin and what I had wanted to do with it. She could've used it to pay for my coffin, but instead, she tucked the napkin and its contents next to my broken body before closing the lid."

"Your daughter learned about integrity from you."

"So you understand now why I can't leave this world and enter God's kingdom to join my Sunny. I need to take care of business. I've spent years searching so I could return Mistress Coulter's gift, and now you can help me."

"I really don't have a clue what you're talking about. Why me? This has to be a dream."

"No, you're wide awake. Follow me."

The image floated through my door, and I opened it to follow. Quietly we descended the stairs and moved into the hallway. He passed through the dining room door, but I had to enter more conventionally. The door of the old buffet swung open slowly. The little man settled on the top of it and, from his pocket, withdrew an object wrapped in a forest-green napkin. "Take it."

I couldn't help doing as I was told. I reached out and what was a foggy image turned solid and grew in size in my hand. I gasped and jumped back.

"Don't worry, unwrap it," he assured me.

Again, I did as I was told. I gently lifted the end flaps and rolled out what lay inside. What lay dazzling before me was a silver soup spoon. It had a plain rectangular handle, and the very center of the bowl was engraved with a simple but elegant rose. Why did it seem so familiar? I knew I'd seen something like it before, but where?

Again, that little image of a man seemed to read my thoughts and spoke, "Open the wooden box that your momma insisted you take. I bet you have not looked in it since the day you stuffed it here." I just stared at him, not entirely sure where this was going.

Slowly I squatted in front of the open door of the antique buffet and pulled the old box toward me. My mother had insisted that I take the canteen of my great-grandmother's silver. I remember her snapping, "You don't have to use it. Your kids may want to, or you can sell it and buy what you need."

I forgot it was so heavy, but my little man floated down and effortlessly lifted it to the table for me. I pulled out a chair and sat down, ran my right hand over the dusty cover, and took a deep breath before lifting it off. Inside were loads of odd bits of old tarnished silver. I began rummaging through the box, not sure what I was searching for. At the very bottom, in the far right-hand corner, were assorted teaspoons. I put my hand on something larger than the rest of the pieces.

"That's it. Take it out!" he whispered.

Slowly I raised the piece high to catch the light from the hallway, and as I did, the tarnish fell away and the piece glimmered. It was an exact match to the one the little man had handed me. I glanced at the little man, who beamed and nodded his head. "Ms. Lizbeth Coulter, here is what your ancestor, Ms. Betty Ann Coulter, loaned me so I could be free. I give it back to you so I can be truly free."

With that, a gentle breeze circulated the room. The distinct colors of the man mixed together, and a multicolored diffuse light raced around the dining room, creating a slight breeze before heading toward the fieldstone fireplace. He floated up the chimney, and all that remained was a string of fading "thank you's" that soon grew into silence.

DESERT DISCOVERY

Marcy inserted the old key into the equally ancient lock of the motel room. She had to slightly lift the door by the knob and jiggle it a bit in order to get the bolts to release. TripAdvisor sure was correct about the Desert Oasis: "Modest, tired rooms that needed updating years ago. Clean and cheap." She threw her backpack onto the bed, not worrying about dirtying the threadbare bedspread, and made her way through the obstacle course of eclectic furniture toward the tiny bathroom. She knew that a shower would help clear the jetlag and the doubts that remained in her mind.

Despite the shabbiness of the tired bedroom, the shower poured out pounding hot water that worked her muscles and renewed her soul. She felt rather guilty being in the desert and using so much water, so she cut her ablutions to five minutes and grabbed thin, scratchy white towels from the rail. She wrapped her wet hair in one and began drying her body with the other, but she was rudely interrupted with the cell-phone ring that told her Roger was checking on her yet again.

"Hi, Rog, What's up?"

"I just wanted to make sure you had arrived and that everything was all right."

"What do you mean 'all right'? All right that you weaseled out of this trip? All right that I can still manage to enjoy a trip without you?"

"Oh, stop it. You know I meant that you arrived safely in that little town. Can't remember the name. What are you doing anyway?"

"Let's see. Check it off, now. I sat on the bowl, had a shower, and washed my hair. I'm going to get dressed and walk across the parking lot for some food. Okay with you?"

"Yup, that's fine. I'll call you in the morning and see if Miss Cranky Pants has disappeared and my fiancée has returned." Roger disconnected without a good-bye, and Marcy threw her phone onto the brown-and-yellow-checked easy chair.

She finished drying herself, combed out her hair, and pulled it back into a ponytail. She threw on cutoff jeans and a pale pink T-shirt and slipped her feet into her favorite sandals. Grabbing her shoulder bag and room key, she headed across the dusty parking lot toward the tiny cantina run by the Desert Oasis Motel owners. The best part of traveling by oneself is that you don't have to cater to anyone else's wishes. Roger hated eating at unrated restaurants that served home-style food. Gourmet dining at multi-starred establishments was his thing. She loved small, tucked-away places because it was a great way to meet locals, learn the ins and outs of an area, and try new foods. She sighed as she pushed open the screen door and looked around the tidy, unpretentious dining room.

"Hello. Welcome to Mama's Cantina. Do you want a table for one?" asked a smiling plump woman about her age with the darkest brown eyes Marcy had ever seen.

"Well, yes. It is just me, myself, and I as you can see," snapped Marcy.

"I am so sorry. I didn't mean to offend you. I just meant do you want to sit at the counter or a table. Please forgive me," explained the earnest young woman with cocoa eyes and shoulder-length black hair.

"I guess I'm the one who should apologize. Sorry for being short-tempered. The counter will be fine, and then you'll have the table if a larger party comes in."

"No problem. I'm Carmella. Come and choose whatever seat you want while I get you a tall glass of ice water. Lemon?"

"Carmella, that would be lovely," responded Marcy with just a hint of a smile on her face.

She moved toward the counter, where two stools were occupied by lovesick teenagers and one by a National Park ranger who was enjoying a piece of piled-high peach pie with a scoop of ice cream. He nodded, acknowledging Marcy as she sat a few stools to his left, and she in return said, "Afternoon."

Carmella arrived with a tall, frosty glass of water and a handwritten menu. She noticed Marcy's surprise and added, "My mother changes the menu every week, depending on what fresh foods are available, so we handwrite them."

"Wow! That must be a pain."

"I agree with you, but Mama insists on working that way. She likes the old ways, which includes using only local fresh foods. Some of our regulars hate that they cannot rely on their favorite dishes being available, but others love the changes. I'll give you a moment to look it over. Don't hesitate to ask if you have any questions."

"Thanks." Marcy studied the menu, trying to decide what to have, when her problem was solved by the ranger, who was readying to leave.

"Go for chicken mole. Mama makes her own sauce from a secret family recipe. Her grandmother also made it, according to my father. It is the best in the state of Arizona."

"Sounds great! Thanks for the tip! Chicken mole it'll be!"

"Enjoy your stay."

Marcy waved good-bye to the friendly man. Within minutes, Carmella arrived with a plate of chicken mole, rice, and beans.

"I heard you telling Bill you'd try it. Here you go. Enjoy."

"I'm sure I will."

The chicken was the best Marcy had ever had. It was tender, and the sauce was spicy with just the right amount of chocolate. Both the rice and beans were freshly made, she was sure. As she scraped the very last morsel from the plate, Carmella remarked, "I see that you didn't like it. Come back tomorrow and maybe you'll find something more to your liking."

Both women laughed. "Oh, I'll definitely be back. I'm here for a week to get my desert fix, as I call it. I just can't get enough of the colors, landscape, plants, and animals. My soul revives here, and unfortunately, my fiancé doesn't get it. So I'll soak it all in and then go back East."

"That's a shame," remarked Carmella. "You have to be in the desert to learn to love it. Maybe he'll come with you next time."

"And maybe hell will freeze over."

Once again, both women laughed, but this time until tears filled their eyes. Marcy reached for her wallet to pay her bill and handed the cash to Carmella. "Thank you for making me feel so welcome and for the laughs. I needed it. See you tomorrow. Have a good night."

"Sleep well, my new friend."

Marcy went right to her room and had the same difficulty turning the key. *I'll have to tell the desk clerk in the morning that the lock needs attention.* A quick change into boxers and a T-shirt and brushing of teeth was all she could manage before falling into a deep sleep. She slept soundly until the ring of her phone shattered her dream of a nocturnal hike in which she was confronted by a mama javelina teaching her baby to forage for food.

"Hello?"

"Morning, Marcy. Did I wake you from your beauty sleep?"

"Yes. It is two hours earlier here. Remember?"

"Forgot. Sorry. What are your plans today?"

"I'll grab some breakfast at the cantina across the way. Food is fabulous and all local. Really kind people. Then I will head into the park, grab a trail map, and—"

"You're really going to hike by yourself? Do you think it's safe?"

"Well, had you decided to come as planned, I would not be alone. Forget it. I hiked alone before I met you, and I guess I'll continue to do so. I'll call later."

Marcy disconnected and silently wished she was on an old-fashioned landline so she could've slammed the receiver down to show how she really felt. She threw the bedsheet off and stormed into the bathroom, feeling completely exasperated. No shower, save water; just a strip-down wash will suffice. Once calm and clean, Marcy dressed, filled a small day pack with snacks, binoculars, sunscreen, and a light jacket and headed out for breakfast.

The counter was full of early risers, but one seat was free at the far end. Marcy glanced at the customers as she made her way to the stool, noting that everyone seemed local. Sign of good food, as far as she was concerned. As she sat, a smiling young man who did not look more than fifteen met her with a pot of coffee.

"Coffee?"

"Thanks. I take it black. Could I please just have a couple of fried eggs and toast?"

"Sure. No problem."

Marcy slowly inhaled the java fumes and then sipped what she considered to be the nectar of the gods. She reached into her bag to pull out the preliminary information she had downloaded about Saguaro National Park. She had background info about the park, a driver's guide to the Cactus Forest Loop with suggested stops detailed on the back, and a map which did not seem to scale.

"Rats."

"Have a problem?" asked the young man as he delivered a plate brimming with sizzling hot food. "Can I help? I'm Andrew, by the way."

"Marcy. Oh, I was looking for guides to hiking trails, that's all. I'll get some at park headquarters. This looks delish, thanks."

"I think I've one in my jacket. I'll look for you."

Before Marcy could say a word, he headed off to what appeared to be a staff room. In seconds, he was back, smiling broadly, and handed her a much-used hiking guide. "Here you go. You can take it with you and bring it back tomorrow at breakfast."

"Thanks! I'll just check it out while I eat."

By the time Marcy was ready to pay her bill, she had a tentative plan for the day but decided to check in with the visitors' center first. She filled her water bottle from the pitcher Andrew had so kindly left, paid cash as it came to a whopping $7.75, bid her new cantina fans a cheery good-bye, and headed for her car.

She wended her way into the park, stopping at all pullouts to get a good view of the Tanque Verde Peaks. The beauty of the early morning in the desert never ceased to amaze her. The colors were muted blues, purples, and reds; and the sand sparkled as the sun slowly rose higher. *There is nothing like the peace of the desert to revive one's soul,* she thought. She finally arrived at the visitors' center twenty-five minutes into the drive and was happy to see the same ranger she had met in the cantina the previous night was on duty.

"Well, hello again. Did you try the mole?" He smiled.

"I sure did, and it was the best. Thanks for the recommendation."

"How can I help today? I am Bill Perkins, by the way."

"Pleased to meet you, Bill. I'm Marcy. I just wanted to go over my plans with you as I'm traveling solo. I was going to pull in at Mica View and walk down the Mica View Trail, continue east on the Shantz to the Pink Hill Trail, and then return on the Javelina Wash. What do you think?"

"That will be a good four miles. Make sure you have plenty of water because it gets mighty hot quickly out here. Oh, also be on the lookout for Gila monsters. They're cute but poisonous. A few have been seen and some pack rats' nests have been disturbed, and we think they might be the culprits. Have a great time, and I think there will be some great pork enchiladas with green sauce on the menu tonight. It'll be a good bet."

Marcy laughed. "Thanks for all of the tips, hiking and culinary. See ya."

The ranger waved and she was off. It was all she could do to keep driving to the parking area without ten million more stops. The dirt road leading to the trail head was wide and, despite a few holes, was well packed. *Oh please, do not let this be a sign that there will be hordes of people here,* she thought. She was relieved to see there were only spaces for a dozen or so cars, and she was number 3 to arrive that day.

Marcy, an experienced hiker, rechecked her pack to make sure she had the liter of water, trail mix, banana, and cheese. She double-checked that she had put in the map the ranger had given her as well as sunscreen, a pocketknife, and a first aid kit. When she was convinced she was well prepared, Marcy slipped her phone into her back pocket, locked the car, and attached the keys to the loop inside her pack.

It was great to be out early before the crowds and the sweltering sun. The trail was obviously popular because of its width, but it still seemed unspoiled. The cacti and other flora were beginning to bloom, but the luscious white blossoms atop the saguaro were slow. An occasional one had opened, and that surely would make the bats happy. Saguaro blossoms were their favorite food. The flowers on the branches of the Palo Verde were ablaze in yellow and did an excellent job of sheltering the younger saguaros.

As she ambled along the path, every change in scent, every tiny blossom, every cactus, each with its own adaptation for desert survival, brought a smile to her face. She paused with each new birdcall, identifying some and wondering at those sounds she did not recognize. *How could anyone not love this place?* she thought to herself. *Roger just doesn't get it, and truthfully, he doesn't even want to try.* She shook her head and continued on to the Pink Trail, drinking in every sight, smell, and sound. Lost in thought, she could barely manage a wave when people walking toward her greeted her. She kept pushing lingering thoughts of Roger away with the beauty of her surroundings.

She felt twinges of hunger as she reached the intersection with the Javelina Wash Trail and checked her watch. Well, no surprises, it had been a few hours. How could that be? She started down the trail and soon came to a bend where a huge Palo Verde's branches overhung a patch of saguaro. Perfect place to stop for a bit and a bite.

Marcy removed her pack, checked the immediate area for creatures that would not appreciate her presence (such as scorpions and spiders), and had a seat. She unscrewed the cap of her bottle and enjoyed a swig of the cool water. *These Sigg bottles are just the best*, she thought and closed her eyes for a few minutes to center her thoughts. She realized just how grateful

she was to be in this amazing place. *No one can take this from me;
it's a part of me.*

She shook her head and took out her bits of lunch and arranged
them next to her. She again carefully checked the ground for
possible snakes sunning themselves on the hot ground, insects,
and Gila monsters before settling down. Clipping the cover
of the pack closed, she turned to put it behind her to use as a
backrest but leapt to her feet, feeling spooked by what she saw.

Who would leave a backpack here? This is weird, and why a spade? She
looked in all directions, grabbed her binoculars, and double-
checked for signs of other hikers. Not even footprints. She
shrugged her shoulders and admonished herself not to be a
wimp. She settled down and slowly enjoyed every delicious bite
of her cheese, banana, and trail mix, followed by gulps of the
fresh, cool water. A couple—probably seniors—made their way
toward her and stopped.

"Good afternoon. Fabulous place, isn't it?"

"Oh yes. It sure is. Of course, any place in the desert is fine
by me."

"Ah, and you even managed to find a bit of shelter from the sun
for your lunch. Do you come here often?" asked the gentleman.

"Never enough, but maybe I will change that. Are you visiting or
resident to the area?" inquired Marcy, rather surprising herself
with the question.

"We've been in Arizona for close to twenty years, so we are
almost considered residents by some," responded the woman.
She laughed. "But to others, we are still newbies and will always
be so."

He quickly added, "But we love it here and will never leave. We walk in either of the parks every day unless the temps top 100, and then we stay inside and safe. Well, nice talking with you. Stay safe."

"You too. Hey, by the way, you don't know anything about that pack, do you?" She pointed behind her. "It was here when I arrived, and it seems a bit odd."

"No, someone will come back for it," assured the gentleman.

Marcy stood, packed her leftovers back into her day pack, and checked that she had left nothing behind. She glanced at the pack and spade, shrugged her shoulders, and headed down the path to complete her hike. When she reached the car park, she saw there was not one vacant space.

"How was the hike?" asked a ginger-bearded man exiting the beat-up Corolla parked next to her.

"Great! Spectacular flowers and views across to the mountain range. Getting hot though, so be careful."

She waved, leapt into her car, and shut the door to avoid any more conversation. Marcy started the motor, blasted the AC until the car cooled enough to humanly bear the heat, lowered the windows, and backed out of the parking slot. She drove slowly down the access road, glancing from side to side, not wanting to miss anything. She had to slam on the brakes to avoid a pair of roadrunners scooting across her path. This brought a smile to her face and a sharp reprimand to stop brooding and enjoy the moment.

She completed exploring the circular drive around the Cactus Forest, making several of the recommended stops. She really wanted to hike along the Loma Verde Loop so she could see the bajada, the gravel plain at the base of the mountain, but decided to play it safe with the heat. Maybe tomorrow she would get up early, grab a piece of fruit, and explore it before breakfast. She stopped to pick up a taco and iced tea from the cantina to take back to her friendly little motel room. Her new BFF, the park ranger, happened to be there too; and seeing him jogged her memory.

"Hey, I enjoyed my hike."

"I thought you would."

"But there was something a little strange. I was sitting, eating a snack at the beginning of the Javelina Wash Trail, and there was an abandoned spade and green backpack—a JanSport like kids want for hauling books to school—just sitting there. No signs of people. I think it was next to a pack rat's den from how you had described them to me. Thought you might want to know. Anyway, I am looking forward to a siesta in my cool, albeit noisily cooled room. Have a good afternoon. See ya."

"Thanks for the info. I'll have one of the rangers check it out."

When Marcy woke from her afternoon nap, she could not believe that she had conked out for two hours. She smiled and stretched—pure relaxation. *Be fair to Roger. Call him,* she thought to herself. *Don't just bitch that he hasn't called you. Call him.* She reached for her phone on the night table and instructed Siri to call Roger.

"Hey, good afternoon, sweetheart. How's my favorite desert rat?"

She cringed. "Great. Had a fabulous walk, saw nature at her best, and met lots of friendly people. How are you?"

"Hey, be careful talking with strangers. You never know—"

"Stop it. I'm perfectly safe. I've even become moderately friendly with a park ranger and told him about the backpack."

"What backpack? What are you talking about?"

"The one I found abandoned on a trail."

"Oh, Marcy. You aren't sticking your nose into where it shouldn't belong again, are you?"

"No, Roger. I have to go, speak to you in the morning." Without waiting for a reply, she hit the END button and cut him off. She leapt to her feet, waved her fists above her head, and screamed,

"That man will drive me to drink!"

Marcy spied her guidebooks and trail maps and settled into the rather battered chair to make a plan for the next day's adventure. As she pushed back her head to operate the mechanical footrest, she noticed a remote. She picked it up, inspected it, and laughed, thinking it should be in an antique shop as it looked just like Grandpa's. She clicked on the old Magnavox for company and resumed her search for tomorrow's adventure. The local news began, and her head shot up when she heard the question: "Does this backpack look familiar?"

"Yes! That's like the one I saw," she shouted out loud and then felt rather foolish.

The news commentator continued, "This backpack was found in Saguaro National Park along the Javelina Wash Trail. It contained the silver spoon pictured, some sand, and a small handheld spade."

"No, the spade was beside it!"

"If you have any information or know to whom it might belong, please contact the Ocala sheriff."

Marcy turned off the television and took a deep breath. *Whoa, what did I find? Ah shit, I better call because Ranger Bill knows I know about it.* With the decision made, Marcy did a quick search for the correct number and hit CALL.

"Sheriff Babcock here."

"Hello, my name is Marcy Lannon, and I just saw the clip on the TV just now. I was the person who told the park ranger about the backpack. I saw it when I was hiking today and thought it strange."

"Well, hello. Thank you for contacting the office. I sure would like to talk with you. I can come to you if you'll tell me where I can find you."

"Sure, I'm staying at the Desert Oasis. Do you know it?"

"Everyone in these parts knows the Oasis. Best food in the state. I'll be there in ten."

Marcy barely had time to wash her face and comb her hair before there was a firm, loud knock on the door. "Coming," she yelled from the bathroom. Checking the peephole, she saw a tall, lanky man in uniform with a traditional star badge on his chest. He had his hat in his hand, revealing a buzz cut. She removed the safety chain and opened the door.

"Evening, ma'am. I'm Sheriff Rick Babcock. I answered your phone call. I assume you're Marcy."

"Yes, sir."

"Why don't we chat over at that circle? The octillion is flowering and hasn't dropped its leaves yet. It's a lovely evening and heat isn't too bad. I'll meet you there."

He turned and ambled toward the wooden Adirondack chairs that so badly needed a coat of paint. *I like this man,* thought Marcy. *He wants me to be comfortable with him.* She grabbed her sunglasses and room key and followed him.

He remained standing until she reached the circle and then indicated that she should choose a seat. Once she was settled, he removed his jacket and put it on the back of the battered wooden chair. He joined her, extended a hand in welcome, and then pushed back in his seat with hands behind his neck. His muscular arms were revealed, as was the pistol that hung from his belt.

"So where do you call home?"

"Oh, I'm from the Boston area."

"Come to escape the freezing weather and snow that I've been hearing about?"

"Not really. I just love the desert. It may sound corny, but I truly revive my soul here. I love the peace, soft light, and smells."

"But you're on your own?"

"My boyfriend doesn't get it. He likes hustle and bustle and bright lights. So I traveled on my own before I met him and guess I'll have to continue to do so in the future."

"Too bad. So will you throw me out if I tell you I'm a Yankees fan?"

Marcy laughed so hard her stomach hurt. "No, but if you tell me you have cursed my boys of summer, I may. We members of Sox Nation are fiercely loyal."

Now it was the sheriff's turn to laugh. "So, have you been to Saguaro before?"

"No, but I have spent a few vacations in the general area, down around Douglas and Bisbee and also in Organ Pipe National Park."

"Not many visitors go there. You must be pretty dedicated to exploring the desert."

"That would describe me perfectly."

"So tell me about the pack and spade you saw."

"Well, I ran into Ranger Bill at the cantina over there where I got a snack. Didn't he give you the information?"

"Yes, but I'd like to hear it from you. After all, you were there." He slowly smiled.

Marcy shifted in her seat, took a deep breath, and repeated the details of her hike and how she discovered the pack at lunchtime. She emphasized that she thought it strange to see an old green JanSport type of pack and spade there.

"Were there any tracks? Signs of disturbance?"

"No—no human tracks, for sure. I had seen the orientation video at the visitors' center before I went into the park and had chatted with the ranger. From that, I would say because of the assorted dried vegetation and the upturned sand, there was a pack rat's nest that had obviously been disturbed. Nothing else that I noticed."

"Now why did it make you think it was a pack rat's nest? Not many East Coast people would know that."

Feeling exasperated by his lack of confidence in her, she replied, "Dried vegetation, rocks, piles of dirt, shiny stuff. You know, I don't need to tell you. There were mounds like that all over the park. There was even one with tracks leaving it on another trail. Before you ask, four walking feet and a tail, dragged along."

"Got it. Why did you choose to sit by that particular saguaro?"

"Oh, I had heard a Gila woodpecker and stopped to watch it pecking away in a cluster of young cacti growing under a patch of Palo Verde trees. I wondered how long it would stick at it, and as I was getting hungry, so I decided to sit down and eat while waiting it out."

"Did you touch the backpack or look in it?"

"Of course not. It didn't belong to me. I knew it was out of place, but probably wouldn't even have said anything about it had I not run into Ranger Bill or seen that bit on the news report. I didn't see the spoon the news guy said was inside it."

"I see. So no one near it? No possible owner?"

"No. I chatted with a few day hikers who passed me, but that's it.

"Okay, Ms. Lannon?"

"Yes, Marcy Lannon."

"How long will you be staying in the area, in case I have any more questions?"

"I leave in three days, but you have my cell if you need me. Why are you looking for the owner?" she inquired. "I suspect there's something more to this than it seems."

"Well, there may just be. We work with all the law enforcement agencies in the area, and I'm not free to give any more information. We'll be in touch if we need you. As you said, I have your number."

The sheriff stood and extended his hand. As they shook, he wished her well for the last days of her vacation, thanked her, and made his way to his car. She watched as he started the engine, waved, and left the parking lot. *Well, that's that,* she thought and returned to her little room. Marcy perused a few more guidebooks and carefully studied her maps of the Rincon Mountains, choosing the next day's possible hikes. She put her materials down, and her thoughts drifted to the news broadcast and what the sheriff had said. *There is something strange about all of this. Dad would have said, "Something is definitely fishy in Denmark."* She grabbed her hoodie and headed for the door to cross the parking lot to the cantina.

Pulling the room door closed with a bang, she noticed the bats swooping across the darkening sky. One finally landed on a flowering saguaro that stood at the edge of the road, and she followed it. *Must be a lesser long-nosed bat,* she thought, remembering what she had just read. She watched it devour the tasty treats from the blossom and was blown away that she had seen this little miracle of nature. Still focused on the greedy little bat, she walked backward toward the cantina. She didn't notice the edge of the narrow dry wash, and she went down in a heap.

She cried out in pain and burst into tears. "Oh my god. It hurts like hell. Help! Help me!" she called out. Realizing that there was no one within earshot, she knew she would have to hobble either to the cantina or her room. Slowly she pulled herself toward the poorly lit cantina, which was a hair closer, and stumbled through the door with a cry of pain.

"My god, what's happened to you? Stay there," shouted Carmella from behind the familiar counter.

Marcy did as she was told, and Carmella was at her side with a chair in seconds. She yelled "sit! sit!" and grabbed another chair on which to prop Marcy's leg. Again, she ran off and returned with a bag of ice and applied it to Marcy's ankle. Marcy winced with the pain and explained what had happened.

"I was watching a bat feast on nectar and wasn't paying attention. I missed the dry wash and fell. I really may have done so damage."

Marcy removed the ice pack, and the women gazed at the multicolored grossly swollen ankle.

"Doesn't look good," commented Carmella.

"Doesn't feel good," responded Marcy.

Both laughed and cemented their friendship. Marcy replaced the ice on her wound and began thinking about her options. Carmella touched her shoulder and said, "Hold on, I'll be right back."

Marcy nodded and had a quick chuckle as she went through the list of possible comments Roger would make about her little accident. *He wouldn't get that it was worth hurting myself to see that bat feed. He'd lecture me that I should have stayed on a solid, well-maintained path.* She was shaking her head when Carmella returned with her handbag and set of keys.

"Come on, my friend. Mama is here, and I called Andrew. He's coming in to help her while I take you to the ER."

"Oh, Carmella. You don't have to do that. If you could kindly go and get my car for me, I can drive myself. It's my left foot."

"You'll do no such thing. We don't treat our visitors and friends like that around here. I'll take you, especially in case they give you painkillers. So let me help you down the step."

Realizing that no was not an option, Marcy whispered a "thank you." She was grateful for the support getting into the car and shut her eyes as Carmella drove to Community Hospital and pulled up right next to the emergency door. Carmella pointed a finger at Marcy, threatened her with death if she tried to get out on her own, and leapt out to grab a wheelchair. Within seconds, she was back, opening the passenger door and lending support as Marcy maneuvered into the chair. She wheeled Marcy into the reception area and left to move the car.

Marcy was neatly parked by an empty chair in the waiting area when Carmella returned. There were several other people waiting—some with obvious illnesses or injuries and others less so. Carmella's eyes darted around the room, acknowledging the locals that she knew and assessing the visitors who had obviously spent too much time in the usual desert heat. She lightly touched Marcy's arm and said, "The wait shouldn't be too bad."

The pain was so severe Marcy could only offer a weak smile and say "From your mouth to God's ears."

It only took five minutes for Carmella to fall into a light sleep. Marcy thought, *The poor woman never gets to sit down. Maybe it's good she brought me.* She picked up a magazine and flipped through a few pages but found it nearly impossible to concentrate on the print, so she slammed it down. She began studying the waiting ill and injured and tried to figure out what had brought each to the ER. Was anyone as stupid as she? It was then that she noticed the man sitting across from her, who had a bandaged hand raised way above his head. Their eyes met.

"Waiting long?" she asked.

"Not too long. I should've come in this morning when it happened though, instead of waiting. That Gila monster gave me one hell of a bite. Now I'm paying for it. This hurts like crazy and is getting really swollen," he explained, bending over in obvious pain.

As he did, a soup spoon fell from his pocket and clattered to the tiled floor. This shook Carmella from her forty winks, and she leaned over to pick up the spoon. As she did, she showed it to Marcy. "Oh, look at the delicate rose. Isn't it pretty, Marcy?" She handed it back to the man and said, "Lovely spoon."

"Thanks."

The man was called into the examining room by a medical assistant, and then the penny dropped. *Gila monster. Silver spoon.* "Carmella, did you watch the news?"

"Marcy Lannon?" the medical assistant interrupted.

Marcy dutifully raised her hand and was then whisked away. It only took forty-five minutes for her to be triaged, x-rayed, diagnosed, and fitted with a temporary air cast until the swelling subsided. Carmella leapt to her feet when Marcy was wheeled out, holding up two fingers. "Two broken bones in my ankle, my friend. I come back in two days for a hot pink cast once the puffiness is gone."

Carmella raised her arms with open palms, shrugged, and went to get the car as the medical assistant wheeled Marcy out. Their path crossed with another worker who was pushing a male patient to a set of elevators. She recognized him immediately as the man from the waiting area.

"Hey, how did you make out?" she asked, not totally out of concern for his well-being.

"Okay, but need to spend the night for observation and some IV prednisone. Thanks for asking."

"Well, good luck. Stop messing around with those Gila monsters."

He smiled and raised a hand to wave as the elevator doors slammed shut. Carmella pulled up to the door and, with the help of the assistant, placed Marcy gently in the passenger seat. As the women made their way back to the inn, Carmella took charge. "I'll drive you right up to your door and see you settled. Then I'll go and see what Mama rustled up for specials and bring it to your room."

"Oh, Carmella, you already have done so much for me. I'll eat at the cantina and then crutch myself across the parking lot to bed."

It took one stern look from her new friend for Marcy to sink into silence and accept all the assistance offered her. Once the car pulled up to the room, the patient was able to hoist herself up and make her way to the door with the aid of spanking new crutches. Carmella put her hand out for the key and then led the way to the comfy chair and footstool. Marcy collapsed into the chair and mouthed a silent "thank you" before Carmella turned on the rackety air conditioner and headed for the cantina and dinner for two. Although it was a good half hour, it seemed only seconds before she returned carrying a tray of hot food and a bottle of cooled white wine.

"Hey, girlfriend, look who the cat dragged in."

Sheriff Babcock followed Carmella into the room. "Hello again, Ms. Lannon," he said and offered his hand. "I was having dinner over at the cantina and heard you had a little accident. So sorry."

"Thanks. No big deal. I should've looked where I was going instead of at that damn bat! A few broken bones in my ankle. I guess this means I need to change my hiking plans for tomorrow."

"Sounds like a good idea, unless you're an expert on those sticks," he replied, pointing at the crutches. "Carm tells me that you met an interesting character while waiting to be seen at the ER."

"Oh, I sure did. And had the park ranger not told me about pack rats, and had I not seen the news—well, it would have meant nothing to me."

"Please, eat. Don't let Mama's enchilada get cold. They have a great kick."

In between bites and sips of wine, Marcy described the man with the hurt hand and repeated what he had to say. Carmella was able to describe the spoon she had picked up in detail. When asked if it was the same as on the evening news, she had to admit to the sheriff she had not seen the broadcast but had been told about it by Marcy. He looked toward Marcy and raised his eyebrows, looking for verification.

"Hard to tell if it was exactly the same. But it sure looked similar, and they both had a rose engraved on the bowl. I couldn't be 100 percent sure."

"Well, thank you ladies. I'll bid you a good night and perhaps be in touch." The sheriff left quietly, and the women were able to finish their dinner, exchanging information about one another and laughing over their similarities and differences. The conversation was only broken with the sound of Roger's distinctive ring on Marcy's cell phone. She shook her head and reacted with "Why he won't let me be, Carmella?"

"I'll go and leave you to share your day. Sleep well."

Before Marcy could respond, Carmella was out the door with the dirty dishes and rubbish. She took a deep breath and reached for the phone and hit the redial button.

"Where were you, babe? Why didn't you answer? Why haven't you called?"

She spoke slowly and distinctly. "Hello, Roger, and how was your day? It couldn't have been more exciting than mine."

"Why do you say that? What's up?"

"I managed to have a fabulous hike, see amazing animals, and meet charming people." She continued, "I may have helped the local sheriff solve a crime and managed to break two bones in my ankle. Can ya beat that?"

"OK, you have me, but I'm not too happy that you're involved with the cops. Not happy that you broke bones either. I bet you were doing something silly too. How did you get medical help in the middle of nowhere? Why didn't you call me? I'll fly out tomorrow."

"No! No, you will not fly out here, Roger. I managed breaking my ankle doing what I love in a place that I love. I have new friends here who took care of me and continue to do so despite my protests that I could manage myself. I wouldn't change any of this other than falling. I'll be fine. As far as the sheriff is concerned, you have no idea what's going on. I'll call you when I get back East. I'm turning off my phone now. Don't call."

Marcy slammed the phone onto the side table and made her way to the bathroom. She was surprised to see a smile on her face when she looked into the mirror to floss her teeth. She finished her bathroom routines and hobbled to her bed for a much needed sleep. She couldn't tell how long she had been sawing logs when she was woken by the general ringtone on her phone.

"Hullo?"

"Good morning, Marcy. It's Sheriff Babcock here. Sorry to wake you, but I thought you would want to know this right away."

"Morning, Sheriff. What's up?"

"Wanna thank you. If it weren't for you, the mystery of the park would not have been solved."

"What mystery?" asked Marcy, who had pulled herself upright.

"Come to the park headquarters with me. The superintendent wants to tell you and thank you. I'll pick you up, as you're not 100 percent. Can you be ready in ten?"

"Make it twenty and you have a deal."

"Great, see you soon."

Marcy put the phone down and hobbled to the bathroom. *I'm getting better at this,* she thought as she managed to wash and dry herself without holding on to the edge of the sink. She was able to dress by sitting on the edge of the bed and finished gathering this and that for her handbag before the sheriff knocked.

"Morning, Sheriff. Thanks for picking me up. Could you just pull my door shut, please?"

"Sure thing. How about you call me Rick."

Marcy made her way to the passenger side and noticed that he had thought to open the door for her before he knocked. She shook her head and smiled. Once in the car, she saw two cups of coffee in the holder. The sheriff seemed to read her mind and said, "Thought you'd want a cup, so I stopped by the cantina. Andrew knew you liked it black."

"Oh, thank you so much, Rick. I need my java wake-up," she replied as she reached for the cup.

They drove to the visitors' center and made small talk, sharing stories about growing up and how both came to love the desert and its people. Those few tourists who were milling around the visitors' center stared but kept their distance as the sheriff went to Marcy's door, opened it, and offered a hand.

"We've got a meeting with Ranger Perkins," Sheriff Babcock informed the cheery park volunteer.

"This way please."

The duo was led behind the desk to an inner office. Although she was never formally told, it didn't surprise her one bit that Bill Perkins was the park superintendent. He rose to shake hands.

"Good morning to two of my favorite people. Sorry about the fall, Marcy, but I cannot thank you enough for alerting us—the police, I mean—to what you saw both in our park and at the hospital. You solved the mystery of disturbed pack-rat nests for us."

Sheriff Babcock interrupted, "And led us to the silver that was stolen from the Historical Society. So we both thank you."

She looked from the ranger to the sheriff and back again. "I'm not with you," responded a very confused Marcy.

The ranger pointed a finger at the sheriff and nodded for him to begin.

"You see, five or six months ago, the Historical Society was robbed during the hottest night we've seen in years. Didn't even dip into double numbers, so most people had left their air conditioning on and windows closed while they slept. It sure was a night no one would hear unusual noises. The thieves took lots of very old documents regarding land grants, fossils, and the silver collection that was owned by the Ochoa family, descendants of Estevan Ochoa."

"Who?" Marcy asked.

"Estevan Ochoa was an early settler here. He had a vast mercantile business. When the Confederacy spread this far, he refused to do business with them, stating what he had achieved because of the US government, and he vowed he would stay loyal to the Union," explained Ranger Bill, whose expertise was Southwestern history.

"Cool dude," replied Marcy.

The sheriff continued, "A few weeks passed, and then we found the most important papers when they were taken to a pawnshop in Phoenix. The owner insisted on holding on to them to have an authority check their authenticity. The slimeball left the documents and went off for lunch, saying he'd be back. Well, it didn't take long for the shopkeeper to find out the documents were stolen, and the police were in the shop when the guy returned from lunch. He saw the cops and took off as if his clothes were on fire. The silver was still missing, but thanks to the good curator at the Historical Society, we had detailed descriptions."

The sheriff pointed at the ranger, and he took over.

"Over the past two weeks, we observed that many pack-rat nests had been disturbed. If it was one or two, we would've continued to assume that our Gila monster population was growing because pack rats are among their favorite food. But this happened over so many days. Our rangers looked closely, and they soon realized they were not destroyed in the way that a hungry Gila typically would have attacked a nest. Couldn't figure it out, but we were beginning to think a human may be guilty of destroying park property and alerted the sheriff. After we retrieved the backpack and trowel that you saw, we found the spoon inside and thought this must be related."

"I'm still not with you," a bewildered Marcy commented.

"Okay, here is the kicker," began the sheriff. "I went to the hospital to talk to that guy you told me about. I told him I was investigating the Gila monster bite on behalf of Animal Control. He just had diarrhea of the mouth. He told me he'd been poking around the nest under the saguaro because he'd never seen a pack rat and wanted to get it to come out. He put his pack down and leaned forward when the Gila monster darted toward him from behind and latched on to his hand."

"Boy, he was stupid, wasn't he?" she commented.

"In more ways than one. I looked up on that rolling tray table that goes over the hospital bed, and sitting there was a spoon with the rose on it. I remarked that the hospital served meals with fine cutlery these days. He said 'Oh, this? This belongs to me. It's a new acquisition.'

"I told him, 'My wife, Rose, who—by the way—really does not exist, would love that for her spoon collection. Where did you find it? Did they have any more?' He responded that this was the only one. I said, 'Gee, that's funny. It's an exact match to the one we found in the backpack that was left in the park near a saguaro.'

"He just looked long and hard at me. Then he said he thought, when I walked into his room, that the gig was up. He said he was sure I knew he had been searching pack rats' nests for the booty his brother had hidden after the heist. His brother thought it was the perfect place to store it because everyone knows those critters liked shiny things and wouldn't question it if items were found. The only problem our friend had was that his brother never told him in which nests to look.

"So the sheriff was able to make an arrest, send deputies to find the brother, and retrieve more items from the Historical Society heist. And the park service solved the problem of perturbed nests," the ranger said as he smiled and leaned back in his chair.

"So I guess my mother is right yet again?"

Both men looked at Marcy. "We're not with you, Marcy," remarked the ranger.

"My mother's answer—whenever we were frustrated by an event—was that everything happens for a reason. We just may not know what the reason is at the time. Had I never reported the backpack, broken my ankle, gone to the hospital, and struck up a conversation with that guy, you wouldn't have solved your mysteries."

"I guess we owe you, Marcy."

"I second that, Rick," added the ranger.

"Well, if that's the case, help me find a place to live and a job so I can stay here. I have found what I need for me."

The three high-fived and Bill Perkins smiled. "We'll do our best."

THE CHALLENGE

Oh, please don't ask me about 7768, Sandra thought to herself as she pushed her shoulder-length auburn hair behind her ears. *I just haven't gotten to it yet. Too immersed in identifying the eighteenth-century china service right now. Love to skip out on this meeting. Better be pleasant as yearly reviews are next week.*

Sandra calmed herself, straightened her silk scarf, and entered the conference room with the confidence that her Eileen Fisher suit gave her on days like this. She took the remaining seat, put down her clipboard, and readied herself for the weekly update. The meeting room in the curator annex was well lit with natural light coming through inoperable windows that nearly stretched from floor to ceiling, but that didn't stop it from being stuffy and airless. That—with the dark wooden walls and an overweight, boring, monotone director—made it difficult to stay focused during department meetings.

Sandra loved her museum work. That is, the actual work—not the bureaucratic bunk that sometimes went with it. She loved being a history detective and artifact restorer. She loved the excitement of receiving an item, researching its origins, learning about its significance, and making a recommendation as to whether the museum should find the funds to buy it, accept it if it was being bequeathed, or give a polite "no thank you." She loved the trust people put in her—but meetings? She removed her red framed glasses, cleaned them with a tissue from her pocket, and replaced them before the conversation began.

"Sandra, please give us an update on that canteen of silver we were offered last month," requested Lily, the head of seventeenth- to eighteenth-century collections. Lily sat ramrod straight and could stare at you with her piercing blue eyes until you felt like the puppy who peed on the floor.

"Oh, Lily, so sorry. I've been spending ten hours a day on that china that came in. So intriguing. I'm pretty sure that—"

"Sandra, that's fine, but what about the silver?" demanded the gray-haired boss as she reached up to adjust the comb holding her twist.

"I haven't started on it," admitted Sandra as she fixed her eyes on her papers.

"Please do so today, even if it is just a preliminary look. The family offering it to us called again to see if we were interested. They say it's been in the family for over one hundred years and want it to go somewhere that it would be appreciated. I need to call them tomorrow morning, so—"

"Okay, okay," interrupted Sandra. "I'll take a quick peek today. Who knows, maybe it'll just be plate, and then we can just give it back."

Lily turned her attention to a slim middle-aged man slouching in his chair. "Jim, maybe you could look at it with Sandra. Working together, you may just be able to issue a preliminary report in a few hours. Is that okay with you, Sandra?"

Sandra glanced at her colleague and smiled. "Great. Two heads are better than one. I'll ask one of the interns to sign it out to us for eleven thirty."

Jim looked at Sandra and gave her two thumbs up and then turned his attention to the boss. Tipping his head to one side, he fixed his eyes on his boss and affirmed, "Why, yes, Lily. I would love to stop what I was doing to help Sandra out."

Lily nodded, realizing she had not asked Jim for his help in the most professional manner. The meeting droned on, and Sandra had to continue to pinch herself in order to stay awake. Every time she snapped to attention, she felt angry. Not that Jim was asked to help her; he had a photographic as well as an analytical mind and loved a mystery as much as she did. She was angry because she liked to finish a project before starting a new one, and also because she felt as if Lily was pandering to the prospective donor. She felt a kick under the table. She looked at Jim and saw him once again leaning his head toward Lily with raised eyebrows.

"Sorry," replied Sandra when she realized she had missed a Lily directive.

With annoyance in her voice, Lily repeated, "Order lunch in for both of you today, and put it on your expense account. I really need a preliminary report on that collection pronto. Right?"

"Oh, thanks. We'll get right to it." Sandra smiled, thinking about the large corned beef sandwiches that could be delivered by the Corner Deli.

The meeting adjourned, and Jim followed Sandra out of the room. They both removed their jackets and loosened their respective tie and scarf. They took a few steps down the hall, out of earshot of anyone, and then looked at each other and laughed conspiratorially.

"Well, I guess I have to put aside the twentieth-century glass on which I was about to make a breakthrough that would have rocked Lily's world—and you, the china. I wonder why we were pulled for the job," Jim pondered.

"Who knows? Maybe we're known as expert sleuths. Anyway, she signs the payroll, so let's get busy."

They passed near the table where half a dozen interns worked, and most seemed totally absorbed by their assignments. The silence of those ensconced in their work was shattered as Ron barreled into the room, late for work as usual. Unlike the others, who were dressed to impress prospective bosses, Ron wore a Bob Marley T-shirt that had been through the wash too many times and jeans that could surely use some attention. His baby-thin blond hair was shoulder length and, for once, pulled back in a kind of ponytail. He pulled his chair out, fell into his seat, dropped a briefcase, and looked up at Jim and Sandra. With a sheepish expression, he mouthed a "sorry for being late," peered into his briefcase, and began grabbing manila folders that contained papers hanging out every which way.

Sandra interrupted him, "Ron, before you get into all of that, we need you to go to stores and sign out number 7768 to me. If security has any questions, they can speak to Lily. Please bring it to my office, and on your way, please pick up more gloves and soft cloths. Thanks."

"No problem. Consider it done."

Ron shot off like a racehorse flying out of the gate. Again, Sandra and Jim looked at each other and broke into peals of laughter. Heading into her office, they began speculating what could be in the old wooden box and whether or not the task set before them could be completed in a few hours so they each could get back to what rocked their world.

Sandra pulled a menu for the local deli out of her top drawer and tossed it toward Jim. "Here. Choose some lunch and we can give an order to Ron when he gets back. I'll tell him to order it for a 1:00 PM delivery. I'll pay for both of us and put it on my account."

Jim nodded, took the menu, and circled his choice—pastrami on rye—while Sandra busied herself clearing the worktable in the corner of the office. She sprayed it with cleaner and gave it a good scrub, making sure there was no residue there that could damage the goods. Jim watched and then offered, "Want me to circle something for you?"

"Oh yeah. Corned beef on an onion roll. Get us some potato salad and extra pickles as well."

"Got it."

Jim had finished marking up the menu when Ron entered the room. His hands were appropriately gloved, and a neat stack of square soft cloths and gloves were balanced on the oak box. He smiled broadly as he put it down.

"Do you guys want some help? This looks more interesting than the work I am doing for Ed on that old sheet music."

"Not right now. He'd kill us if we stole you, but we'll do it if we need to. Oh, could you please order our lunch for us? Lily wants us to work straight through. Jim has circled what we want from the Corner Deli. Here, take these two twenties to pay and ask for a one o'clock delivery. Thanks, you're the best."

Before he could reply, Sandra grabbed the menu from Jim and the money from her pocket. She handed it to Ron with a second "thank you." He, in turn, snapped to attention, saluted her, and replied "done" before leaving the room.

"Good dog," Jim said as he watched Ron leave the room.

Sandra giggled and moved to the table. The box was in the middle, sitting on a protective cloth, and her laptop was close by. After putting on gloves, she began examining the box. Jim took out the museum camera and took photos from every angle. When he finished, she asked him to hit RECORD on the computer before wearing his gloves.

When he was all set, she reminded him, "We're in this together, so don't wait to be asked for comment just because we're doing this in my office. Just chime in."

Jim nodded and began, "The box is made of oak, probably from late eighteenth century, and is plain except for some 1/8-inch beading along the larger rectangle of both the bottom and the top. It's—let's measure—18 inches by 24 inches and is constructed with dovetail joints and is hinged."

"Stop recording," instructed Sandra.

"Okay, friend, let's take a look at this precious silver. You open it. The project was originally assigned to you," encouraged Jim.

Sandra nodded and slowly lifted the lid. They both stared at the silver that was nestled in the canteen. They both looked at each other, knowing without even touching the goods that this was going to prove to be way more interesting than they had originally anticipated.

Sandra spoke first. "Don't say anything yet. Let's hit RECORD and give very first impressions."

Once they were sure this new recording app was working on the computer, Jim nodded and Sandra began, "First impressions: This flatware is battered and dented. Not abused, but certainly well used. Silver must be pretty soft. Three different types of forks, two kinds of knives, and three of spoons plus serving pieces."

Jim injected, "Handles of each piece are very plain, rectangular, and unadorned. Some pieces have a simple rose engraved on the blade or bowl."

Sandra looked at her colleague and pressed the button once again. She checked to make sure everything was turned off.

Jim couldn't contain himself. "This is weird. I don't think I've ever seen an embellishment on the bowl of the spoon. Have you?" he questioned Sandra.

Equally intrigued, she shook her head no and replied, "Well, how shall we tackle this? Test the silver first or just dig in?"

Jim rubbed his chin and suggested that Ron be given the task to test the silver with acid tests so they could do the fun stuff. She laughed, rang for their zealous intern, and within seconds, there was a gentle tap on the door.

Still giggling, she managed a "come in," and Ron dashed in eagerly. "What's up?" he asked.

"We have a task for you on this job that needs to be done today. Have you learned to test for authenticating silver quality and dating?" inquired Sandra.

"Yes, did it in placements last year."

"Great. Go get all you'll need from supplies and your laptop. If you haven't loaded the app, you'll need to write a report, download it from the server. Then I'll set you up on that end of the table. Okay?"

"You bet. Thanks for trusting me, you two." Ron looked from Sandra to Jim, broke into a grin, and was gone in a flash.

Jim laughed and said, "I think we have an eager beaver. Let's get cracking."

The duo began by taking photos of each type of flatware, recording all dimensions, and inventorying all the silverware. It was grunt work that they hated doing, but it had to be completed. Once it was all recorded on a database, they breathed a collective sigh of relief.

"Let the fun begin," cried Sandra.

"The simplicity of shape and design of each piece and the signs of usage are unmistakably that of the late eighteenth century, don't you think?" asked Jim, looking for confirmation of his beliefs.

"Yeah, but that rose is bothering me. It doesn't fit. It also seems screwy that it's on the blade of the knives and the bowls of the spoons. It makes no sense. You would expect to see that on the handle. Jim, you said you've never seen it, but have you ever heard of a spoon with an embellishment on the bowl?"

"No, can't say that I have. Let me hit a few reference books and Google."

"I'll search and see if I can find a hallmark on any piece. It'll be hard as they are battered and so tarnished."

They worked in silence, each absorbed by their individual challenge, so much so that they did not hear Ron enter the room and set himself up at the other end of the large table. When he was organized with the paraphernalia for testing some of the pieces and the app was opened on his computer, he loudly and purposefully cleared his throat.

Sandra's head shot up. "Oh, super, you're all set? Need any help?"

"No, I'm ready to go." He showed his gloved hands and pointed to the end of the table.

Sandra scraped her chair as she rose and went to look at his setup. Satisfied that he had everything he would need, she returned to the canteen; removed a knife, spoon, and fork; and brought it back to him. "Here you are. See what you can tell us."

Sandra returned to her seat by way of the closet. She grabbed nitrile gloves to protect her hands, some non-ionic detergent and distilled water (which would carefully clean any dirt and grime from the silver), and a 30X jeweler's loupe. With a sigh, she wondered if this would do or if she would have to beg some time from the labs to use their electromagnetic tools. She grabbed a spoon and began the meticulous work.

Slowly and methodically, she rubbed it with a soft cloth, pausing to make sure no damage was being done. Occasionally, she dipped a swab into the solution she had made with the water and detergent and gently swiped an area of the spoon. Sighing, she flipped it over in her hand to try to clean the bend on the back of the handle near the bowl. With the loupe still lodged in her eye socket, she pushed back in her chair, let out an "oh shit," and beckoned for the guys to join her. Jim and Ron looked up from their individual work and scrambled to her side.

"Tell me I'm not seeing this," she demanded as she pointed to a faint, but certainly discernible, blocked PR. "Pull up hallmarks from the eighteenth century, Ron."

Ron reached across the table for his laptop and, within seconds, located a PR. "Look! It's right here. You are seeing it, sister. From my testing so far, I can tell you that it is eighteenth century and is solid. The composition looks as if it is 91.6 percent silver weight, which would be correct for our man."

Sandra nodded. "OK, I have a plan. I'll keep going through these pieces. Maybe the larger ones—the serving pieces—have one of the other hallmarks Revere used. You guys see if you can uncover anything about the roses."

The men nodded and pushed their laptops together. All three were working so intensely that they didn't hear Kelsey, the senior intern, deliver their lunch. "Hey, you guys, it's time to come up for air!"

"Can we eat while working?" asked Ron. "I want to keep going."

Both conservators shook their heads. Sandra rose, removed her gloves, and pointed at her desk. "Gentlemen, let's chow it down in record time."

That is exactly what they did. Within ten minutes, lunch had vanished; all three had scrubbed their hands and were back at work.

The men were searching books and Internet records for anything that would provide information about the engravings. They murmured to one another, pointing out bits of information and making notes on a large yellow pad of paper. Sandra continued carefully cleaning pieces, searching for more hallmarks. Finally, she removed a pie server and flipped it over in her gloved hands. She began the swabbing process and watched in disbelief as some block-lettered words slowly became visible.

She looked up at the men and again called them to her side. "Guys, come see this."

In seconds, they were by her side. They grabbed gloves and eye loupes and huddled in to study what she had found. Popping eyes and open mouths accompanied a few mutterings of "oh shit." In small, even block letters, the words PAUL REVERE were just visible. All three pushed back at the same time and took deep breaths.

"Okay, guys. Well, that is established, but what is with the rose on some pieces? Is there any record of this in what you have seen?"

"Not yet," replied Jim, "but I'm going to call Jen over at the Paul Revere House right now."

An hour passed with Sandra on the cleaning and searching for marks, Ron searching the Internet, and Jim in conversation with Jen. The intensity of the work was interrupted when Sandra's phone rang.

"Yeah, Sandra Malone here. Oh yes. Hi, Lily. We may have some initial good news. In fifteen minutes? Umm, okay. We'll be there."

Sandra looked up at her coworkers and beckoned them to join her. Ron, of course, was there in a nanosecond while Jim held up a finger.

"Thanks, Jen. This initial info is incredibly helpful. So it would be okay if I worked in your archives for a bit tomorrow? Great! See you then." Jim put down the phone, pushed back, and let out an almighty "YES!" before joining the others.

"It seems our man occasionally did special orders for people, whether he approved the design or not. Jen's best guess is that someone either loved roses or had Rose as a name and wanted to be able to see the rose as he or she ate instead of covering it with a hand. She's going to search some archives, and I'm going there tomorrow to look through everything she has. What's up?"

"Lily in fifteen," replied Sandra. Three pairs of eyes rolled.

The three put their heads together and decided who would say what. They high-fived one another as they left Sandra's office, practically skipping their way to Lily's sanctum. Jim gently knocked as Sandra was holding the old oak box. Once an unenthusiastic, barely audible "come in" was heard, they piled in together, laughing amiably. Lily had arranged chairs around the small round table on which a protective cloth had been placed in the center. That was where Sandra placed the canteen, and they all took a seat.

"Well, what do you have?" Lily asked.

Sandra began by explaining how they divided the work and what each one of them did to unlock the mystery. She opened the box and offered a few pieces to her boss once her hands were gloved. As each detail was given, Lily would either nod, let out an "oh" and nod ever so slightly, or just listen intently. She never interrupted the excitement of the museum detectives, just let them spill out every little detail of what they knew and what they still needed to find out.

"So, let me sum this up from my perspective," began Lily. "You have before us a canteen of flatware that was made by Paul Revere—or someone who worked for him—that was a special order. It is well used but of excellent quality. The mystery remains as to why there are roses engraved on the blade or bowl of some items, with some possible answers over at the Revere House. Right?"

"You've got it in a nutshell, Lily."

"Okay. So I see there seems to be a few pieces missing in the box. Any guesses as to why or how many are AWOL?"

Sandra took a deep breath. "Well, if we assume that place settings were complete, we can make a guess at the numbers. Give me a minute."

Sandra donned gloves, grabbed a paper and pencil, and began counting and making notes. The others chitchatted quietly so as not to disturb her. In five minutes, Sandra looked up and said, "OK. I reckon there are six teaspoons, one demitasse spoon, and four soup spoons missing. There are three spots where I bet there were serving spoons with nothing there. I wonder when they went missing and where they are now. I bet there are stories to be told as to where they have been, don't you?"

The other three shook their heads in agreement. The eager beaver jumped up and down with excitement. "Yeah! Let's find those damn pieces!"

Lily laughed at Rob's infectious enthusiasm. "Good work, guys. I'll call the family, and tomorrow, you can get more info on the roses. And, Rob, be a good dog and find the story of the missing pieces."

There are so many people to thank! T. M. Murphy, you inspired me to write and let my imagination fly. You pushed me to allow what I know to seep into the stories and to add more details and mystery to my work. Sarah Murphy, you were copy editor extraordinaire. Thank you, family and friends (too numerous to mention), for reading early versions and encouraging me to keep going. Lindsey Dawson, thank you for always wanting to hear stories, especially memory stories, as you were growing up. Finally, Mick Dawson, thank you for being the most supportive, loving husband and friend a gal could have. I am blessed!